"Wake up, Lissa, for God's sake!"

Lissa instantly jolted awake, startled by the urgency in Grant's command. She glanced over at his handsome profile, outlined in the glow from the plane's instrument panel, and her heart flipped crazily.

"The storm's closed in," Grant said curtly. "It's too dangerous to fly now. I'm going to try landing."

Lissa tightened her seat belt, her thoughts melodramatic but strangely calm. Grant had made her feel so very alive—and now they were going to die together! She looked at him grappling with the bucking plane as they went through an updraft. Emotion made it difficult for her to speak.

"Darling, I love you!" she cried out chokingly.

Had he heard her? She had no way of knowing as the ground suddenly came rushing up at them....

SHEILA STRUTT
is also the author of these
Harlequin Romances

2333—THE MASTER OF CRAIGHILL
2447—ON THE EDGE OF LOVE

Many of these titles are available at your local bookseller.

For a free catalogue listing all available Harlequin Romances
and Harlequin Presents, send your name and address to:

HARLEQUIN READER SERVICE
1440 South Priest Drive, Tempe, AZ 85281
Canadian address: Stratford, Ontario N5A 6W2

Stamp of Possession

by

SHEILA STRUTT

Harlequin Books

TORONTO • LONDON • LOS ANGELES • AMSTERDAM
SYDNEY • HAMBURG • PARIS • STOCKHOLM • ATHENS • TOKYO

Original hardcover edition published in 1982
by Mills & Boon Limited

ISBN 0-373-02496-7

Harlequin Romance first edition August 1982

CHAPTER ONE

'CUT! Okay, people, that's a wrap! Let's move on to the next location!'

The premonition had been there all morning, lurking uneasily in the recesses of her mind, but at the sound of the old familiar litany, repeated in an aggressive Cockney accent by a fattish man wearing a blue peaked cap, the muscles in Lissa Benson's throat clamped tight. She swallowed to clear them. What was she so alarmed about? She hadn't known there was filming going on in Masseyville, but why should it bother her? The past was past. The present was what should concern her now: a trip to the beauty counter of the local drugstore to find out what she could do about turning herself back into the well-groomed young woman Ramsay had last seen when she had seen him off at the airport on his way to Mexico: the perfect picture of a rising young oil company executive's future wife.

The film company started to gather itself together like an army on the march with cast and crew and cameras instead of soldiers and tanks. Lissa crossed the wide main street to keep well clear of them. Her premonition that something was going to go wrong had been ridiculous. All that could go wrong was that the drugstore would be

out of her particular brand of cosmetics and
nothing could be done about the light dusting of
freckles across her nose—something that definitely
did not go with Ramsay's image of her.

She went into the air-conditioned drugstore,
colder than winter after the brilliantly hot and
sunny street outside. Bill Massey had a lot to
answer for. When the job as his secretary in this
out-of-the-way part of prairie Canada had presented itself three months earlier, she had expected
to spend most of her time in the farm office, but
Bill was childless and liked the company of young
people, so most days he had tempted her out with
him, riding or driving across the ranch.

Waiting for the store clerk to attend her, she
caught sight of herself in the overhead security
mirror. A tall, five-foot-nine-inch girl with shoulder-length auburn hair and the sort of figure that
looked good in skirts or pants. The mirror was too
far away to pick up the greenish-grey of a pair of
wide-set eyes or the slightly stubborn set of a chin,
inherited from her father, that put her face on the
squarish side of oval but, all in all, it was a passable
face, Lissa decided—except for the freckles.

'May I help you, ma'am?' The store clerk had
finished with her other customer and came up to
her.

Lissa flushed, something that came easily in spite
of her summer tan; embarrassed at having been
caught studying herself so openly. She ducked her
head and fumbled in her purse. 'Yes,' she said, 'I've
got a list!'

She need hardly have worried about not getting what she wanted, she reflected, as the pile of name brand products grew on the counter in front of her. What was more to the point was if she had enough cash to pay for everything she'd bought or if she would have to fall back reluctantly on her credit card. But most of the generous salary Bill Massey paid her was still in the bank—and Ramsay was worth it, she told herself.

'Oh, and I'll have a packet of emery boards as well,' she said as the clerk started to put her purchases through the till.

By the time she left the drugstore with a weighty bag of purchases in one hand and a much lighter purse in the other, she had practically forgotten about the filming, and a sudden surge of people along the sidewalk took her by surprise. While she had been inside, the unit had moved to a new location just opposite the store and when a woman pushed past, anxious for a front row place for this novel entertainment, she stepped back, awkward and off balance, catching her heel in a crack in the pavement. She stumbled and might have fallen if a hand had not come out and caught her arm.

'Thank you!' Preoccupied with getting the bag more securely lodged in the crook of her elbow, she still had no idea, then she looked up and her stomach clenched. This, then, had been the cause of her premonition.

'Think nothing of it!' The voice was just as disturbingly familiar as the face; deep and resonant, its pitch controlled by the diaphragm and not the lungs and capable of the merest sibilant whisper or the roar of towering rage. 'Where are you going?' it went on.

'Back to my car—but I can manage.' She tried to pull her arm away, but the fingers tightened, steering her past the crowd in the opposite direction.

'I'm sure you can!' The eyes above her glinted in the sun, echoing the vocal irony. 'However, Fate having taken the trouble to bring us together, don't you think she might be more than a little offended if we didn't make the most of our opportunity?'

'I don't have time.' She tried to pull away again. 'I have to go.'

'I'm sure whoever's waiting for you will understand when you tell them that you had no choice.' The reply was as smooth as the grip was powerful. 'We'll go this way—there's a coffee wagon round the back.'

She had no choice except an awkward, embarrassing scene as he propelled her past the crowd and then drew her back to walk her quickly along the street, thigh brushing thigh and all feeling focussed on the touch of his fingers against the bare skin of her arm. But even so, people were already beginning to look curiously in their direction, half identifying the face so many of them had seen on the screen.

It belonged to Grant Ferries, one of the best known film actors in the Western world and one of the very few Canadians who had made it to the very top. Lissa knew it by heart. Strong planes, almost harsh, and a jutting nose above a thinly curved mouth. It was a cruel rather than a handsome face, but the cruelty was sensuous and had him voted, year after year, as one of the top ten male box office draws.

It was almost impossible not to know anything about Grant Ferries. The magazines were full of him. Grant Ferries with yet another aspiring film starlet on his arm, entering or leaving a premiere. An action shot of his latest film; true life stories of his life and loves. Anyone who had ever stood beside a magazine rack at a supermarket check-out would have found it difficult to avoid seeing something about Grant Ferries.

'We go round here.' Once around the corner away from the crowd, the pressure on her arm seemed to relax and she tried once more to break his grip.

'I don't have time!' she repeated desperately.

'And I say you have!' He glanced down at her without breaking stride and her breath caught in her throat.

Although the face was so familiar, she was still unprepared for the total shock of his eyes. They were a deep cobalt blue, and heavy lids, used to such devastating effect, gave the impression that he could pierce the protective covering of skin and bone and read the thoughts beneath. A look in close-up from the screen had millions of women believing that he was looking just at them. Their effect, combined with a deeply tanned skin and thick blond hair, now grown to a point just below his ears, was irresistible.

He noticed her response and smiled, a flash of strong white teeth against his tan. 'There's always time for things that are important,' he said. 'Besides, we have to talk.'

He turned her again, this time into an enclosed hotel parking lot that had been cleared of all vehicles except the film crew's cars and trucks and a coffee wagon in one corner.

'I've nothing to say!' Lissa responded angrily. 'Especially to you!' She might not be able to resist him physically, but she could resist.

He stopped and swung her round to face him. The scar was still there, she noticed. A thin, almost imperceptible white line, running from the corner of his eyebrow to his hair.

'In that case, you must be unique among women!' He was smiling but he was definitely not amused. 'If I were to believe my own publicity—which heaven forbid!—I would say that half the female population of the world would give their eye teeth to be where you are now!' The bantering stopped abruptly. 'We're going to talk, and the only choice you have——' relief flared and died, 'is if it's going to be here, or if we're going to have a coffee and be a little more discreet.'

Lissa glanced around. They were standing in the middle of the yard and some of the film crew, also straggling in for their morning break, were already beginning to glance curiously in their direction as they stood rigidly at arm's length.

It was no use. 'I'll have a coffee,' she said,

defeated. 'But I warn you, I have nothing more to say!'

'We'll see.' With a last look, he released her arm and strode off in the direction of the coffee wagon, automatically assuming she would follow.

She toyed with the idea of running, but discarded it as quickly as it came. Where had she got to run to, except the Masseys' and, if he wanted to, Grant Ferries would have no trouble in tracing her there. In a small town, everybody knew everybody else. The first person he stopped on the street would probably be able to tell him where the auburn-haired girl with the English accent lived.

She followed him towards the coffee wagon, despising herself for noticing and reacting to the breadth of shoulder under the faded denim shirt and the long muscularity of hips and thighs thrusting against the close-fitting jeans. He took his place in the growing line of technicians ready for their coffee break; one of them and yet somehow one apart. There was arrogance in the tilt of his head, and authority. He might be wearing the almost universal working uniform of shirt and jeans, but he would never merely be one of a team. He was a loner, an individual; a man who set his own challenges and lived up to them.

She went and stood a pace away from him. Some of the crew exchanged casual remarks as they went past and the script girl came up to him, checking a detail for the shooting later in the day and shooting more than a curious glance at Lissa, but Grant himself took no more notice of her until they were under the striped awning of the coffee wagon and one of the cooks inside was looking expectantly across the counter.

Then he turned to her. 'Do you want something to eat?'

'No, thank you.' Food would have stuck in her throat.

'In that case,' he looked back at the cook, 'two coffees, Gordie.'

'Sure thing!' The cook put two full styrofoam cups on the counter. Grant added milk to one, picked up the sugar, hesitated and put it back.

'Here you are.' He handed Lissa the un-sweetened coffee and picked up his own black one. 'Over there should do!' He nodded towards a corner of the yard which, as if by common consent, had been left empty. The less glamorous side of filming, crew members found anywhere they could to take their coffee breaks when they were on location, sitting on walls or leaning back against the hoods of parked vehicles, but although there were two canvas directors' chairs and an empty folding table, no one had gone over to that particular corner.

Lissa followed him across and sat down, feeling her face hardening as the silence lengthened. Most women would have given their eye teeth to be in her place, he had said, and so might she at one time, but now she was older and life had taught her too many painful lessons. He had got her there with his film star arrogance, so let him start the conversation.

But even so, it was she who first reached break-ing point—sipping her coffee, looking anywhere but at him, but all the time feeling the insidious power of those eyes stripping away her outward defences, even down to the light print dress she wore, until she felt naked and totally exposed.

Finally she broke. 'What are you doing here?' she asked ungraciously.

His head went back on his corded throat, arro-gant even in victory—a look she had so often seen before. 'We're doing background shots for a film about the Riel rebellion,' he answered casually enough. 'Things haven't changed around here too much in the last hundred years if you shoot to miss the cars and the television aerials. We go up north next month to start the main production work.'

'In the winter?' Keeping the conversation to the film might be safe.

'Sure. I want authenticity. It's my first film as a producer, so I intend to give the public that at least. Had you heard?' There was a pause.

She picked up her cup. 'What?' she asked evas-ively.

'That I'd gone into production?' He challenged her to deny that she knew what was common knowledge, but how could she deny it? 'Star Turns Movie Mogul!' 'Ferries Wheels and Deals!' Grant was one of the best known Canadians in the world; even the regional prairie newspaper had carried headlines.

'Yes, I'd heard.' She despised herself, but she despised him even more for forcing her to admit that she had even that amount of interest in him. But everyone had read about the Anglo-Canadian production company he had formed to spearhead Canada's thrust into the international motion picture industry and about the woman he had chosen to play the only significant female role in an otherwise all-male cast. 'Will acting the part of his wife lead to real wedding bells?' one female columnist had cooed.

'I'm pleased to see you're well informed.' He leaned back in his chair and studied her, satisfied.

'It's difficult not to be,' she said ungraciously.

'Yes, I guess it is!' He went on watching her through half closed lids, part taunting, part hypnotic in a way that she remembered so very well until, with an immense effort of will, she broke the spell.

'I have to go.' She put down her cup.

'Not so fast!' He stopped her easily. 'There's one more thing. I need a secretary, and I'm offering you the job.'

Lissa was horrified. 'I'm afraid that's quite impossible.' She wouldn't work for him if he was the last man on earth.

Forgetting about the fragile nature of the table, she stood up. The table began to topple and a hand came out and caught it and another gripped her wrist, so that suddenly, instead of being feet apart, she was in his arms, thigh against thigh, breast against breast, drowning in a sea of memory; seventeen again and longing to be kissed.

It took the sound of approaching footsteps to

make the outside world come crowding back.

'Another popsie, Grant?' The leering whisper was just loud enough to hear. It came from the man with the Cockney accent she had noticed in the street: paunchy, with hot eyes under the peak of his trendy cap, he was making no secret of looking her up and down.

To anyone who didn't know him well, Grant would have seemed untouched, but she could see the sudden rush of anger tightening the tiny muscles in his face and when he spoke, his voice was glacial.

'No,' he said, 'my wife!'

CHAPTER TWO

BARBADOS! The shoreline was always perfect at this time in the morning. As it was so few degrees north of the Equator, the sun always rose and set at six, or a few minutes either side, and at six-thirty every morning Melissa Jane Benson was down on the beach. Usually she had it to herself, the tourists not having yet shaken themselves free of the effects of late night dancing to the steel bands, but this morning she was not alone.

She had seen him in the distance, hazy and somehow brooding in the heat already beating up from the white sand, but when she came out from her regular morning swim he was much closer and most certainly not hazy. The sun behind him was turning every hair of his closely cropped blond head into single strands of silver-gilt and his shoulders and slim hips were clear cut against the frieze of motionless palm trees farther along the beach. He was wearing an unbuttoned short-sleeved shirt over his brief bathing trunks, and muscle stood out in a strong, symmetrical pattern on his stomach and chest, but although he was by no means the sluggish white Lissa associated with newly arrived package dealers, neither did he have the angry tan most tourists had within a few days of their arrival.

No, he wasn't a tourist, she spontaneously decided, but on the other hand, he wasn't a resident, either. Island society was tight-knit and she knew everyone, at least by sight.

'Good morning!' He had stopped a few feet away from her, at the end of a solitary trail of footsteps stretching back across the sand, and his voice confirmed her intuition. It was Canadian; nothing unusual about that—a lot of visitors to the island came from Canada, but it was different. Calm and authoritative, with none of the hasty diffidence with which the rare early morning tourist tried to scrape up an acquaintance to last him through a two-week holiday.

'Hi!' She squinted up at him—unusual in itself now that she had grown so tall—standing with one hip thrown out and one long, tanned leg slightly bent. A girl in a woman's body, with an ungainly schoolgirl stance.

'I'm surprised to find anyone here so early. I thought I would have had the beach to myself!' And that, he implied, had been his intention. A solitary, early morning walk along with his thoughts, as the sea turned from grey to pink to a dazzling aquamarine blue.

'I come down here for a swim this time every morning!' Lissa stopped. Her mother was always warning her that she shouldn't be so trusting of strangers, but Lissa had always laughed. With fourteen of her seventeen years lived on the island, she knew almost everyone, and those she didn't know—here she generally shrugged—well, she could always take care of herself. She always had in the rough and tumble on the beach with local boys her own age whenever the accidental intimacy of barely clad bodies had triggered off a look or touch that was suddenly not so innocent. But with this man, she was no longer sure. He was a lot older than her teenage friends, in his mid-twenties at the very least, and although nothing had been done or said, she was suddenly acutely aware of the brevity of her bikini and of the water glistening on her suntanned skin.

She turned awkwardly, looking for her towel. 'I have to go.'

'To school?' Quicker than she, he bent and picked it up and handed it to her, and yet, in spite of the speed of his reaction and of the strong toes gripping the sand, there was awkwardness in his movement, almost a limp. There was a scar, too. A thin red line from his hair to his left eyebrow, lifting it slightly and giving him a sardonic look, but underneath that look, the face was tired; weary to the bone. Something behind Lissa's breastbone stirred.

'No, I don't have to get ready for school.' To hide her vague feeling of uneasiness, she started towelling her hair and then, remembering, she quickly wrapped the towel around her bikini and tied it in a sarong, her fingers working with the speed of long practice while her mind wrestled with the small mystery of that movement within her breast.

'For work, then—or are you on holiday?' He had fallen into step beside her, taking it for granted that he should walk with her towards the bungalow perched on the shallow cliff.

'Neither.' She laughed and the constrictions eased. All that had probably happened was that her stomach had woken up and was demanding breakfast. She laughed again, enjoying how good it felt. 'I live here,' she nodded towards the pink-washed bungalow with its wide verandah draped in bougainvillea, 'but I left school last summer. I go to secretarial college now.'

'I didn't know Barbados had such a thing.'

'Oh, yes!' She looked up, quick to defend and totally unprepared for the impact of eyes above her own so intensely blue that the Caribbean stretched out behind them became a pale, Atlantic grey. 'It's in Bridgetown,' she said jerkily. 'Just a small one.'

'And you live here?' He glanced up at the house

above them and her breathing settled down.

'Yes,' she said.

'In that case, we'll probably be seeing each other again.' He smiled and some of the weariness left his face. 'I'm staying with friends just along the beach.' He nodded past the hotels where bus boys were already beginning to set out loungers and sweep all traces of yesterday from the sand ready for a new day's sunworshippers. The villas beyond the hotels were set in their own grounds; mostly owned by non-islanders, and all owned by the well-to-do.

'I see.' Lissa turned back to find him watching her and once more felt that curious tightening behind her breast.

The eyes held her with a brilliant piercing blue. 'What's your name?'

'Lissa—no,' she corrected quickly, 'Melissa Benson.' This was an occasion where her full name seemed appropriate. 'I'm sorry,' she flushed, 'but I have to go. Goodbye!' She ran up the rickety wooden flight of steps to the bungalow, a picture of flying arms and legs and hair. He was already walking away when she looked back.

She never saw him on the beach again and his absence began to grow on her. She found herself staying a few minutes longer or going down a few minutes earlier, always telling herself it was for some other reason but knowing it was always because she hoped he would appear.

But why should she be concerned about someone who had probably changed his mind and left the island? Life was fun, particularly in the high tourist season from December through to April when the hotels were in full swing, and particularly now she was seventeen and had her parents' permission to go dancing at weekends on palm-fringed dance floors underneath the stars with her group of friends. And although shorthand was hell, Lissa decided, typing was much easier, and there were days when she could actually imagine herself as a secretary when her course finished the following July.

What she couldn't tell was how much she was changing. Fining down so that the bone structure broke through, giving her a face dominated by wide, enquiring green-flecked eyes in a creamy, tanned complexion and adding a grace to all her movements that had not been there before. And the change wasn't all physical. Boys she had known and admired all her life suddenly seemed callow and a little immature. There were even times when life didn't seem such fun.

'Have you heard who's staying with the Campbells?' Her mother addressed the question to both of them one night; Lissa sitting at one side of the dining table and her father at the head.

'No? Who?' True to form, George Benson could not have sounded less concerned. Much older than his wife and on the verge of retirement after a life as a schoolteacher, first with the Army and then in what had once been British colonies, he had already drifted more than half way into the world that was his real interest—books. Except for his wife, people—even Lissa—took second place.

'That Canadian racing driver, Grant Ferries,' Lily Benson said. 'You know, the one in all the papers who had that dreadful smash. He's been recuperating with the Campbells, apparently. That's why Sylvia hasn't been to bridge—she's had to stop in and look after him. Not that she did all the nursing herself, of course,' she smiled at the thought of wealthy Sylvia Campbell changing sheets, or worse. 'But apparently he had a relapse soon after he arrived and it was touch and go for a while.'

It couldn't be! It couldn't possibly be the man she had met on the beach. Outwardly, Lissa went on eating her avocado, but inwardly she was comparing what she already knew with what she had just heard. The scar, the pallor of his skin, the air of weariness—all these pointed to a man just out of hospital and come to the tropics to recuperate, but underneath it all there had still been the hardness of a man who earned his living dangerously. And then there was Sylvia Campbell. The Campbells had one of the villas he had pointed out.

And while she had been wondering why he had never come to the beach, he had been ill, practically dying, if her mother was to be believed. Now the stirring behind her breast was one of pain. She choked on her avocado and her mother looked across.

'Darling, do take some water! Anyway,' she went back to the subject uppermost on her mind, 'he's recovered now and Sylvia's asked us all to a party she's giving for him Saturday. You, too, Lissa, and you, George, so it's no use saying you won't go!'

The Campbells' villa had been transformed for the occasion. Fairy lights hung in the trees; the classical white neo-Georgian portico had been floodlit and so had the flight of steps leading down from the terrace into the lush tropical profusion of the garden beyond and, behind it all, the sea: a sheet of black oiled silk with a fringe of palms. Even as they walked from their car, the sound of music and human voices drowned out the incessant noise of the tree frogs, and when they got inside it was almost overwhelming.

Sylvia Campbell hadn't invited just the three of them, she had invited the whole island, Lissa thought, as her fifth partner of the evening stumbled across her feet on the crowded dance floor. Grant Ferries must indeed be quite a 'catch'.

Just about everyone she knew was there, the boys all strangely different in dinner jackets with their hair slicked back instead of bathing trunks and jeans, and she was different, too. In honour of the occasion, her mother had insisted on buying her a new dress. Usually, the local seamstress made her things, but this was different: filmy and sea green, hanging from thin shoulder straps and fitting closely rather than with the extra half inch that had always been 'left for growth'. To complement the dress, she had piled her auburn hair on top of her head in a mass of curls and tendrils. For the first time in her life, she felt truly an adult.

Yes, Grant Ferries must indeed be a catch.

She had seen him directly they came in, although at first she had barely recognised him. The man on the beach had been a carbon copy of the man she was seeing now; vibrant with health and deeply tanned in a white dinner jacket which did little to disguise the raw strength underneath. He had been laughing down at the woman at his side and Lissa had recognised her, too: a budding film star with her picture in the island papers when she had arrived for a short holiday.

The ache behind her breastbone stirred again.

'Do you want something to drink?' The music stopped and her partner's smooth, boyish face came into focus.

'Yes—champagne!'

'Champagne? But there's fruit punch out for us.' The face looked worried.

Lissa tossed her head; beyond his ability to cope with in this mood. 'I said champagne,' she said defiantly. 'And if you won't get it for me,' she added as he still hesitated, 'I'll go myself!'

She went to the crowded buffet and picked up a glass and quickly drank it down. She could see her parents playing bridge in the room behind, but there was no sign of Grant.

She had expected him to recognise her the moment she had arrived and her breath had come out in a deflated rush when she had started to go up to him, only to have him turn away and laugh down at the girl clinging to his arm.

But why should she expect him to remember her?

That was when Lissa had sneaked her first glass of champagne. They had met once, two months ago, and since then, although the thought of him might have grown and grown in her mind with all the insidious power of an addiction, he had had other things to occupy him. His illness and now—if she was reading the signs correctly—the arrival of someone much more his style than a teenager he had met once on a beach and mistaken for someone still at school.

And it was so unfair. The partner tonight in whom he was showing so much interest couldn't be more than a year or two older than she was herself, and yet there was a gulf that had nothing to do with years. This girl had the gloss and poise of a creation of a major film studio's publicity machine, right from the top of her shining platinum head to the tips of her tiny feet in their wispy sandals with impossibly high heels that brought her just to a level with Grant's chin. The pain in Lissa's chest had become unbearable and she had reached for her second glass of champagne.

And that meant, with the ones she had had in the intervals between dances since then, that the glass she was now reaching for must be her fifth or sixth.

'I think you've had enough of that, don't you!' A hand came between hers and the full glass on the starched white cloth of the buffet table, striking invisible sparks as it caught her fingers and put them none too gently to her side.

'It's none of your business what I drink!' Seconds earlier she had been comparing herself with his partner and calling it unfair; now she was sounding just like the spoiled, petulant child she had been wishing with all her heart that she was not.

'It may not be my business, but as there's apparently no one else around to keep an eye on you and you're unable or unwilling to exercise any self-control, it would seem to be my responsibility.'

Lissa knew what she would see before she looked up; eyes filled with a hard, blue mocking light and a sensual mouth twisted in a derisive smile. The reality caught and held her with her face just inches away from his. She fought herself free of its effect.

'I'm quite capable of looking after myself, thank you!'

'Are you?' One eyebrow lifted, tugged by the scar which had been an angry red when she had first seen it but was now no more than a thin white line running up into the crisp blondness of his hair. 'I doubt it!' The last vestige of his smile faded as he studied her, lips slightly parted and her cheeks flushed a hectic red. Under the searching pressure of his eyes, the filmy green dress began to melt. She felt weak inside and, in the heat, the room began to shimmer. 'You need some air,' he noticed roughly. 'Come on, let's get you out of here.'

He gripped her by the elbow and walked her around the edge of the dance floor on indiarubber legs. The moment the cool air hit her she collapsed, leaning with her head against his chest, weak and queasy but never more conscious of anyone in her life than the man now holding her gently in his arms.

He didn't speak for a long while, then, 'Are you feeling better now?'

Lissa raised her head under its weight of drawn-back copper hair, looking at him through the rainbow of tears gathered along her lower lids. How could she have been such a fool! Why did she mind so much? 'I'm sorry,' she barely whispered.

'Don't be!' His reply was the exact opposite of what she had expected. 'We all make mistakes from time to time—even you, Melissa Benson.'

Surprise made her stand away from him. 'But I didn't think you remembered me!'

'Oh, yes, I remembered you.' In the soft glow of the fairy lights strung in the Pride of India tree above them, his eyes were luminous. 'I haven't had too much else to think about these last few weeks. What I didn't think was that the next time I saw you, you'd look like this!' He paused and spread his hands to describe the effect of a sea-green dress on a slender rounded figure under a cascade of starlit hair, with satin skin accentuating the curve of full young breasts as they disappeared into the shadows of the closely fitting bodice. Suddenly, the hands were no longer spread apart, but cupping her face as if it was a fragile piece of china. 'Lissa!' Her whole body responded as he whispered her name and she automatically lifted her mouth for his kiss.

Along with the sound of footsteps coming along the terrace, the brush of his lips against her forehead was the biggest disappointment of her life.

'Lissa! There you are!' Her mother's sharp voice completed the process of anti-climax. 'I've been looking for you everywhere. It's time to go!'

The argument about Grant started in the car on the way home. Surely she knew his reputation, her mother fumed, and on top of that, everyone at the Campbells' party must have seen them go out on the terrace alone together and, in her half tipsy state, heaven only knew what everyone had assumed.

She didn't care what everyone had assumed, Lissa retorted, and she didn't know about his reputation. Unlike her mother, the gossip columns in the papers left her cold. She didn't want to know, any more than she wanted to know about the string of beautiful women with whom his name was constantly associated; women like the one at the party with him that night.

As if by telepathy, her mother picked up the thought. 'But I don't know what I'm worrying about,' she concluded. 'Judging by the look on that Morgan Vale's face, he's got more than enough to keep him occupied. We'll probably none of us ever see him again. Darling,' her voice softened, able to be generous in victory, 'don't look so desolate. A man like that isn't right for you!'

He was on the beach, waiting, when Lissa went down the steps the following morning. And he was right, she knew it with every fibre of her being, as her foot slipped and she stumbled on steps that she had been running up and down without a second thought almost every morning of her life.

'Hi! How are you feeling? No sore head?' Even though he was relaxed and smiling with the pinkish early morning light catching his face and hair, the power was still there and the magnetism that had drawn her to him the previous night was just as strong.

'No, I'm fine!' She found herself looking everywhere except straight at him. He was wearing brief dark blue bathing trunks and the muscular body and hard, strong legs aroused her in a way that was both disturbing and exciting. 'Are you coming for a swim?' she asked the palm trees in the distance as she took off the wrap covering her own bikini.

He looked at her. 'Yes. Are you?'

She couldn't answer. Tossing her hair back across her eyes, she ran into the shallow surf and dived into the first curling wave. When she surfaced and looked across, he was beside her, swimming with powerful strokes towards the nearest hotel jetty.

After that, he was always there, either on the beach or on the jetty, watching her as she swam towards him.

Morgan Vale, she heard, had left the island, but he stayed on and they talked about everything; stretched out in the sun on the jetty as the stones beneath them slowly warmed and leaving only when the first hotel guests started to appear. There was so much to know. Books; their favourite things to do; their favourite music. Grant's eyebrows had risen almost as high as her mother's when she had said reggae and Dave Brubeck and not the Beatles.

She was older in some of her tastes than she looked, he had teased her.

Her mother's eyebrows had risen when she heard about these early morning meetings. He was too old, she said. He was merely using her as a diversion to fill his time until he was fit enough to leave the island, but Lissa stuck stubbornly to her morning swims until, quite suddenly, they were over.

'I'm flying home tomorrow.' Grant waited until he bent to pick up his towel, the limp that had been so obvious when they first met virtually gone.

Her stomach jack-knifed. 'Back to motor racing?' was all she could think of to say.

'No, not to racing.' He straightened and spoke quietly. 'I used to think that racing was the only thing worth doing, but since the crash, I'm not so sure. When you think you're going to die, it's amazing how much more there is to life than pushing a Formula One car to its limits. I've had feelers from a film company about acting as adviser on a film they're making about motor racing. I shall probably do that, at first, at least.'

The blonde film star—Morgan Something. Lissa's stomach clenched once more. 'So I shan't be seeing you again?'

'It's not likely.' He was towelling his hair and she couldn't see his face.

'But, Grant, I've got to ... I mean ... ' She stopped as the towel dropped and the full impact of his eyes hit her. 'Can't we have one more swim? How about tonight? You've never swum at night, have you?' she went on with forced brightness.

'You should, you know—the water's like warm silk. Please, Grant!' She was begging. She knew it and she didn't care.

He looked across her shoulder at the people beginning to appear on the beach. 'Okay, then,' he said slowly. 'I'll meet you here at ten.'

She had one more chance. All through that day, all she could think of was that somehow, that night, she had to make him kiss her. When there had been so much time, it had been enough that he had wanted to be with her. It hadn't mattered that, far from wanting to kiss and hold her, he had—it seemed deliberately—kept her at arm's length; careful not to touch and veering away from the occasional subject that might lead on to dangerous ground. But tonight she just had to make him stop treating her like a sister—or like the almost-schoolgirl he had met that first day on the beach. She had changed so much since then that she just had to have something more than the memory of his lips brushing her forehead to take through life as a reminder of the time when she had fallen so hopelessly in love. Once it was out, even in her head, the knot in her stomach loosened, but nothing could take away the feeling of utter loneliness.

'Where are you going?' Her mother looked up sharply at the sound of the screen door closing.

'Just for a walk,' Lissa answered breathlessly, frightened even at that distance that her mother's X-ray eyes would be able to see through her dress.

But they couldn't. 'Don't be long, then—and

don't go too far,' was all she said.

The night was perfect, not a soul about and the sound of the tree frogs fading as she walked down the steps towards the beach under perfectly full moon. She could see him well before she got there, outlined against the slight phosphorescence of the sea and, in the distance, the upbeat rhythm of a steel band.

He was standing with his back to her and she quietly slipped off her dress.

'Is this your idea of a joke?' He spoke roughly, even angrily, when he saw her.

'Everyone goes skinny-dipping at night!' She spoke brightly, but her plan was misfiring badly and she had to struggle to carry it through. It was the only thing she had been able to think of, but she was still totally unprepared for the shock of having a man's eyes on her, naked, for the first time in her life.

'Put your dress back on!' he commanded angrily.

'Not until I've had a swim!' Still trying to carry through what she now realised had been a totally ill-judged scheme, she attempted to run past him into the surf, but he caught her easily, gripping her wrist and holding her rigidly at arm's length. 'Put your dress on!' he repeated.

'No!' Caught between humiliation and bravado, she resisted him.

'In that case, I'll have to do it for you.' He half led, half dragged her towards the outline of the small pile of material just visible against the flat emptiness of the beach.

Lissa fought him until the breath ran out of her: fought until, suddenly, they weren't fighting any more. The accidental sweep of her hair against his face or his hand against her breast, neither of them knew what changed the mood, but she heard the harsh exhalation of his breath and then she was in his arms, all woman against the smooth hardness of his body as he kissed her to the moon that hung above them and then slowly, slowly, slowly, let her float to earth again.

'Okay—now get this on!' He broke the spell by bending and picking up her dress and pushing it towards her. 'And then get the hell out of here!'

It was like a douche of icy water. 'But why?' she choked as the dress went roughly over her head.

'Because I've spent weeks exercising the self-control not to touch you, and I'm not going to have you break my track record now!' His humour was turned against himself, his mouth set in a hard, straight line.

'But I wanted you to touch me!'

'I can see that.' He straightened her collar with a rueful smile. 'Now go on, get out of here!'

'No! I'm not going!' She clutched his hands and held them to her breast.

'Have you any idea how difficult you're making this for me?' He sounded tired.

'And have you any idea how difficult it is for me?' It was hard to speak through the thick moisture gathered in her throat. 'I love you,' she choked, 'and after tonight, I'm never going to see you again!'

He stiffened. 'You're being ridiculous!'

She was suddenly furious. 'No, I'm not! Stop treating me like a child! I'm old enough to know how I feel!'

'Which is how old?' he challenged her. 'Seventeen? In ten years, you'll only just be as old as I am now.'

'And does that matter?' she blazed with wet eyes.

There was a long, long pause and then he took her in his arms. 'No, I guess it doesn't,' he said huskily.

They were married two months later in a quiet ceremony in the garden of her parents' home. Then they flew to Switzerland for a honeymoon and then on to London where they were to make their first home.

In those two months, Grant had gone back to England to tie up the loose ends of his racing career and start preparation for the work he was going to do as technical adviser on a documentary about motor racing, his first film, and Lissa had had to withstand all the pressures that she was making a wrong decision.

'He's too old for you—too experienced,' her mother kept repeating.

Lissa knew what 'experienced' meant. Too many women—endless affairs. Grant had told her something of his life, but she didn't care. It was over now. He wanted her; she knew it every time he touched or looked at her.

'He won't come back,' her mother warned her. 'It was a holiday romance. He'll forget all about you the minute he gets to London.'

But the phone calls and the letters came almost every day; long, tender letters full of reassurance and plans for their future.

'You're in love with love!' her mother finally told her angrily.

'I'm in love with Grant,' Lissa flashed back. 'And no matter what you say, he's in love with me!'

He came back and, on an April morning, with iridescent humming birds darting around a scarlet hibiscus hedge and against a background of a brilliant sea, she became his wife.

CHAPTER THREE

'THIS is your wife? Your *wife*!' In another time, another place, a man with a smoke-filled Cockney voice was repeating the fact incredulously.

'That's right.' Grant's face was expressionless.

'Cripes, mate! I can't believe it!' The owner of the voice might shake his head, but it was true enough. No one here in Canada might know it, but she was Grant's wife. Melissa Benson Ferries. Lissa glanced across at the man whose name she had borne for three halcyon years when it had seemed impossible that their happiness could ever end and then for three more years when it slowly did.

The pressures of Grant changing his life from racing driver to internationally known movie star had been enormous. In some ways he had been right that night on the beach when he had said the difference in their ages was too great. In time, it was only ten years, but in experience it had proved to be a lifetime.

The strain of long separations when he had been away location filming and then, as he had made the transition from technical adviser to bigger and better acting roles in his own right, the tension of knowing that he was spending every day working with other, much more beautiful women, while the studio publicity machine kept her in the background, a shadowy and almost unknown part of his private life. All this had created stresses that she had been too immature and unsure of herself to comprehend. And the stresses had been increased by loneliness. Everyone she might have talked to was in Barbados. There was no one in London with whom she could discuss her growing fears and unhappiness.

The last straw had come when she had arrived back unexpectedly early in their London flat one afternoon and found Grant with another woman in his arms.

Compared to many of the torrid love scenes in his films, it had been innocent; a man greeting an old friend who had flown in from Canada and decided to pay a surprise visit. But the old friend had been Morgan Vale, the blonde film actress who had been with him in Barbados, and Lissa had turned tail and left.

Grant might have seen her standing in the doorway, but Morgan most definitely had not, and she had left without her clothes, without goodbyes, without anything.

And Grant had not pursued her or made any attempt to explain, which only went to show how right she had been. He had grown bored with her. A maintenance cheque had arrived through her solicitor at the end of the first month, but she had angrily sent it back. She had found a job in a shop and she could support herself. There had been no more cheques.

The only strange thing about the next few months had been the way Grant had blocked all her efforts to get a divorce. And it was strange. Parts of their marriage had been deeply satisfying and he was a 'marriageable creature', Grant had once joked for the benefit of a television interviewer—and so, Lissa knew, deep down, was she— so the endless stream of pictures of Grant with one or other beautiful woman on his arm had continued but, for once, the trite and hackneyed saying 'we're just good friends' just had to be true.

So she had gone back to using her maiden name and, like the man still studying them with obvious disbelief written in his eyes, very few people knew that she was still Melissa Benson Ferries.

'Melissa, meet Norris Potter, our director.'

Grant made the introductions, but Norris wasn't listening.

'You could knock me down with a feather, mate!' he said in his fierce Cockney accent. 'When did all this happen? Shall I break out the champagne?'

Grant ignored the question. 'I'd prefer it if you left us alone.'

Norris started to back reluctantly away. 'Sure, sure! You're the boss. But don't forget we've got to get a couple more shots in the can before lunch.' With a last look in their direction he walked off, a trendy middle-aged man in a Beatles cap and a collarless shirt, but Lissa was no longer watching him.

'Melissa!' No one had pronounced her name like that, with that slightly rough transatlantic edge, for almost two years, but it still sent shivers down her spine. It also sent shivers down her spine that Grant had arranged for them to be alone. As if by unspoken consent, everyone else was now leaving the yard to go back to the filming in the street. Even the cooks in the catering wagon had disappeared into the back, busy with lunch for the crew's noon hour break.

'How are you?'

'Fine.' They could have been two strangers talking. Six years reduced to four words. No, eight years, if she counted the two since she had left him.

Looking at him now, she realised he had changed. The blond-haired playboy image had disappeared. The hair was still there, but it was longer now, brushing the collar of his shirt and almost imperceptibly streaked with grey. The creases from his nose to the corners of his unsmiling mouth were deeper and there were fans of tiny lines at the corners of his eyes that had not been there before. But, if anything, the years had only made him more arresting. Before he had just been handsome; now he showed all the experience and authority of a man who had the power to choose what he wanted out of life and take it.

'You've changed.' After a silence that was almost tangible, Grant echoed her thoughts. 'When you left, you still looked seventeen. You must have done all your growing in the last two years.'

'I've had to.' And that was true. First the almost twenty-four-hour days of a full-time job in a florist's shop while she went to secretarial college in the evenings and then the opportunity to leave London, where she had never felt at home, and come to Canada where she had been born and lived for the first three years of her life.

'How are your parents?'

'Still living on the island. Dad's got his books and Mother's got her bridge. I don't see much of them.' She had to be careful, she just had to. This ordinary, everyday conversation was making her forget. Grant had even smiled when she had mentioned her mother and her endless games of bridge; a tiny fan of laugh lines creasing the corners of his brilliant cobalt eyes and making his whole face come alive. The ache behind her breastbone that she had never thought to feel again began to stir, proving, if proof was needed, that the physical attraction was still there. But not the loving—that had died under the constant stream of other, adoring women and the long periods of loneliness. And even if the physical attraction was still there, what did it matter? After this one accidental meeting, she was determined they would never meet again.

'I have to go,' she said abruptly.

'Not so fast!' He caught her wrist, circling it easily with his fingers. 'You still haven't given me an answer.'

'An answer to what?' She didn't have to ask—she knew.

'I offered you a job.'

She wasn't looking up, but she could feel him watching her. 'I already have a job,' she said abruptly.

'Then give it up,' he ordered.

Now she flared up, wrenching her wrist away and rubbing it nervously. 'You have no right to tell me what to do! I don't hear anything from you for two whole years and then you think you can come back into my life and start ordering me around! I've made a new life for myself and you're not a part of it!'

'But you still want a divorce, don't you?'

'Of course.' She had stopped trying since she had come to Canada, reconciled to waiting until the legal time period was up and she could get her freedom without his consent, but she could still remember the endless letters between solicitors in

England with Grant's lawyer continually repeating that 'his client was not willing to terminate their marriage at this point'.

'In that case, you might be wise to consider what I have to say,' her husband continued smoothly.

'Why should I?' she demanded. 'And why should I even think of working for you?'

'I've told you,' he answered only half her question. 'I need a production secretary for this film—and I've heard you're very good.'

It didn't occur to her until afterwards to wonder how he knew. She hadn't gone back to secretarial college until well after she had left him. His friends had not been her friends and she doubted if she had seen anybody who knew them both well enough to pass on that sort of information since the day she had walked out of their London flat. He couldn't possibly have any idea how efficient, or otherwise, she was.

So, 'Thanks for the compliment,' was all she said, 'but I told you, I've already got a job.'

'Which, as I've also already told you, you can quit. Unless, that is,' he paused and looked at her intently, 'there's any personal reason why you shouldn't?'

That was the moment when she should have told him about Ramsay. Ramsay was Bill Massey's nephew and she had met him when he had come to her employer's ranch for one of his infrequent weekends. After that first one, however, the weekend visits had become much more frequent and, just before he had left for his business trip to

Mexico, Ramsay had asked her to consider marrying him.

'Of course there's no reason why I shouldn't leave the Masseys,' she said shortly.

'Then why not?' he taunted. 'I'm offering you a glamorous job—travelling on location, working with the stars. What's wrong with that?'

'Everything,' Lissa retorted. 'But mostly that it means being with you!'

'That wasn't always your reaction, as I remember.' His lips curved in an ironic smile and he swept her with his eyes, not needing her to tell him how many memories that small, suggestive movement brought. 'Are you frightened?' he asked.

'Of what?'

'That once we're together, you might not want to leave again?'

'Of course not!' She rejected the suggestion out of hand and his face which, for a second, had held a softer look, now hardened.

'Okay, then, prove it. Work for me for six months and I'll give you your divorce.'

'You'll what?' She was astounded.

'I'll give you your divorce,' he repeated calmly. 'That's what you want, isn't it?'

'Of course it's what I want!' More than anything else, it was what she wanted. 'But what difference does working for you first make?'

'Let's say it's a way for you to prove you've got me completely out of your system.' His blue eyes glinted.

Of all the arrogant, unbearable . . . Lissa's brain

wrestled to find the word and failed. 'Of course I've got you out of my system,' she retorted. 'Nothing you could do could affect me less.'

'Then you've got nothing to lose, have you?' he said urbanely. 'I'll contact you later and tell you when you start.'

'You can save your time and effort.' She started to walk away. 'I'll never work for you and I'll never change my mind!'

'Lissa!' The amusement in his voice stopped her in her tracks. 'Don't you want these?'

She turned to find him holding the bag of cosmetics she had bought with so much pleasure earlier on. Totally frustrated by her inability to get through to him, she went back and snatched them away, and her last sight of him was of him standing watching her with a smile of supreme confidence on his face.

She was shaking when she reached her car and she sat there until she calmed down. So that was what her earlier premonition had been about. She didn't believe in second sight, but somehow, when she had been driving into Masseyville what now seemed an eternity ago, she must have known that something was going to happen to overturn the carefully planned pattern of her life.

When she finally started to drive through the back streets out of town, she did it carefully. Her inclination was to rush, to put as much distance as possible between herself and the man who, however much she might resent the fact, was still her husband. But that would be dangerous, and she held the Volkswagen back until she was well beyond the city limits.

Why? Why was he doing this to her? He had said it was to give her the chance to prove that he meant nothing to her, but he had said nothing about what she might still mean to him! Surely, surely, he couldn't possibly want her back? No! She shook her head and refused to think of it. Grant no more wanted their marriage to resume than she did. If he had, he would have come after her, two years ago when she had left. He wouldn't have left it to a chance meeting. And as for refusing to let her have a divorce—that was pride; pride and arrogance. No one made major decisions in his life without first getting his approval.

Against her will, she had been drawn into reading an article on the front page of one of the sensational tabloids when she had been waiting in line at the supermarket checkout the previous week. The article had been about Grant's switch from acting to film production. He had demanded complete control over the production, it had announced. One of the few Canadian stars with sufficient clout on an international level to demand such a thing, he had claimed control and he had got it. And his first act had been to cast Morgan Vale in the role of his wife.

Morgan Vale of the blonded hair who had caused her so much jealousy from that very first night in Barbados at the Campbells' dance to the day when the sight of her in Grant's arms had sent Lissa rushing out of their London flat and out of his life. However, although still blonded, Morgan was no longer a film starlet but an actress of considerable repute, so there was every reason why Grant should have chosen her to play the part of his wife. Every reason and, perhaps, one more.

Lissa changed gear with a jolt as she took the side road leading to the ranch.

He was planning to turn acting into reality. He was planning to marry Morgan. That was why he wanted his divorce. Their accidental meeting had been purely gratuitous. Grant had already decided to end the game—his way! There might even be a letter from her solicitor when she got back to the ranch.

There was a letter waiting on the hall table when she got in and the sight of it made her heart flip, but it was from Ramsay. She took it up to her room to read it. He had been delayed, he wrote. The negotiations for Mexican crude oil to be shipped to his company's refinery had hit an unexpected obstacle and, instead of a week or two, his return to Canada could be delayed by as much as a month by the Mexican attitude of *mañana*. She could perhaps go down and spend a week with him, he had written hopefully. His uncle would give her the time off. Perhaps she should; Lissa considered the possibility seriously. Anything that could take her mind off Grant was worth considering.

But she knew she wasn't going to make the trip when she went downstairs for lunch. The job with the Masseys had come along at a time when she had been desperate, and she wasn't going to walk out on it, no matter what anyone might suggest.

'Did you get what you wanted in town?' Wilma Massey looked up as Lissa went into the beautiful, old-fashioned dining room.

'Yes, thanks.' It took her a second to realise what Wilma meant. So much had happened since she had bought the cosmetics that had been the reason for her trip that she hadn't even bothered to look at them since she got back. They were still lying scattered on her bed where she had dropped them when she had sat down to read Ramsay's letter.

'And when's Ramsay coming home? Does he say?' Her employer's wife turned to take some salad from a bowl presented by the Indian house-keeper. 'I noticed you had a letter from him in the morning mail.'

'Probably not for a month or two.'

'As long as that?' Wilma glanced up.

'You don't sound too disappointed, I must say!' Bill Massey's much rougher voice overrode his wife's. He came in and sat down, filling the room not just with his size but with the sheer impact of his personality. To anyone who didn't know them, Bill and Wilma were like chalk and cheese—Wilma sweet-faced and quiet and Bill outgoing and posi-tive to the point of being slightly rude. But to anyone who knew them, even superficially, Bill and Wilma Massey were like two interlocking pieces of a jigsaw puzzle; totally complementary.

And Bill also looked like Grant—or as Grant would look in twenty or so years' time. The same impact, the same roughly sensuous features. Bill could have been Grant's father. Lissa wondered why she had never noticed the resemblance—but then, until this morning, she had always tried not to think of Grant.

But perhaps that was why she had felt immediately at home with the Masseys. There was a kindred spirit that had appealed subconsciously. Bill and Grant were both her type of man.

The only pity was that she and Grant had not turned out to be as well matched as Bill and Wilma, she mused underneath the conversation. And yet, for so long, everything had been so perfect. For the first three years they had been totally compatible. Grant had taught her to be his friend as well as his lover and there had been so much happiness as he slowly made the transition from racing driver to technical adviser in the movie industry. Lissa could almost date the moment when things had started to go wrong. It had been when Grant had been given his first acting role in an American epic about the Le Mans twenty-four-hour race.

If they had started a family, things might have been different. But at first—at eighteen, nineteen, twenty—she hadn't wanted to share him with anyone, not even with their own child, and Grant, ten years older, had not pushed her. It had been the only thing, she once realised, in which he hadn't had his way. And it was just as well. With a child—or two—the break could not have been so clean.

'Well, all I can say is that nephew of mine must be an even bigger fool than I took him for—staying on in some godforsaken spot when he could be here, looking at all this!' Bill's eyes, an echo of Grant's blue under a shock of pure white hair, took in the picture Lissa made against the background of his prairie empire through the window.

'Bill . . .!' Wilma protested at his offhand dismissal of his only nephew and closest relative.

'Bill nothing! The boy's a fool.' He took no notice. 'Now, are you coming out with me this afternoon, girl?'

'I should finish cross-indexing the Herefords.' No longer a prairie greenhorn, Lissa now knew enough to pronounce the name Hurford. Having been born in Canada had certainly helped clear immigration problems when the London-based international secretarial agency had found her the job with the Masseys, but it hadn't helped when it had come to understanding the vagaries of prairie pronunciation. No one had known what she had been talking about the first time she discussed the Massey purebred herd of Hereford cattle and sounded every E.

'Aw, to heck with office work!' Bill stood up and half the light disappeared from the room. 'Clay and I need to take a drive up to the north section this afternoon. You'd best come with us. You'll have plenty of time to finish that darned index with Ramsay staying on to fool around in Mexico.'

They used horses, jeeps and airplanes on the ranch, but this afternoon a four-wheel-drive jeep took them across miles and miles of harvested prairie, already set for winter with the stubble tinder dry and a pale, pale gold under the warmth of an almost-summer sun. Perhaps having spent most of her life in the tropics, which were almost seasonless, Lissa appreciated the short fall season on the prairies more than most, but the hint of a bite in the wind rushing past her face was an exhilaration rather than a warning of the arctic winter soon to come. She had never seen a prairie winter and she looked forward to it.

Bill's foreman drove, a silent, taciturn Indian with black hair streaming in the breeze and the classic, straight-cut features of a full-blooded Sioux under his sweat-stained cowboy hat, Clay Southwind had time for only one person in his life, and that was Bill. They sat there now, deep in conversation about minimum tillage and bushel yield, neither of which Lissa really understood. She might just as well have stayed in the farm office and got on with her work, she thought, looking at their two backs, but for all she was ignored, she still felt more accepted and at home at the Bar-M ranch than she had in a long while.

She hadn't had the dream in which she had somehow been turned into a glass vase and was falling down a chute towards destruction since she had arrived at Masseyville. She had arrived tense, with two years' experience of keeping all her feelings under strict control. She was a damned good secretary and that was all she planned to be. She hadn't cried since she had walked out on Grant, but she cried that night.

Something—Wilma's kindness, tiredness after a long journey, a feeling that she had cut all her links

with home—had combined to create a fierce pricking sensation behind her eyes when she went to
bed that first night. Tears! It had been so long since
she had cried that at first she had not realised what
the pricking sensation was, but she had cried that
night and the tears had washed away the accumu-
lated tensions of two years, and when she woke the
following morning, it had been to a day that had
been as tranquil and serene as she had felt herself.

There had been no more dreams of a crystal vase
falling to destruction, and the following weekend
Ramsay had appeared at the ranch for the first
time. It had seemed as if the gods were offering her
a new beginning and she had seized it joyfully.
Why, oh, why had the gods reneged and brought
Grant back into her life?

The jeep had turned and they were heading for
home and she could see the house in its setting of
trees. It was beautiful, quite unlike the purely
functional barns and outbuildings to one side of it.
Wilma had told her that Bill's grandfather, the first
Massey to come out to the prairies, had built it for
the young bride he had sent for from the East to
join him, and his love was obvious in the amount
of care that had gone into the finely proportioned
rooms.

They had once almost had a house like that. Not
a prairie ranch house of yellow brick with a long
verandah running along the front, but an old
Elizabethan manor, set in a hidden fold of the
Sussex Downs.

'Do you like it?' Grant had stood with her, his

arm around her waist, as they had looked at the half-timbered building under an English setting sun. There had been no money for so long and they had lived first in a small furnished flat and then in an apartment of their own in a high block close to the Tower of London. But Grant had just finished his first major film role and he had found this house. It was a house in which to bring up a family with hidden nooks and crannies and the smell of wallflowers drifting through the leaded windows from an uneven red brick terrace.

'Of course I like it!' She had lifted up her face to him, completely unaware.

He traced the line of her cheek and mouth with the gentle pressure of his thumb. 'In that case, I'll put an offer in to the agents in the morning.'

'And get them to sell the flat as well.' She turned away. There was a summerhouse on the lawn that she hadn't noticed earlier.

'That won't be necessary.'

'Oh? Why?' Intent on her exploration, she still hadn't guessed.

'Because we can afford to keep the flat.'

'But why should we?' Used to the freedom of Barbados, she hated that apartment and was pleased to be rid of it.

'I'll need somewhere to stay in town.'

'While I live here?' She turned, very slowly.

'Would you object?' He took a step towards her, but she backed away. 'It's sensible.' He started to persuade a fractious child. 'Darling, I have to be at the studio by seven when I'm working and I've lines to learn each night. It'll be easier all round if we keep the flat and I stay there during the week and come down here at weekends.'

'I see.' All the pleasure had drained from the afternoon and it came out in a small, tight voice.

'For God's sake, Lissa, what's wrong with you?' His patience snapped. 'I make a perfectly reasonable suggestion and you behave as if I'm planning to lead a double life!'

'Well, aren't you? Isn't that what you want? Oh, not you, maybe,' she caught her breath, 'but that publicity woman the other day made it quite clear that her job would be a lot easier if I weren't around. Was it her suggestion that you should buy a place like this and keep me safely out of sight?'

'I'm not even going to discuss this while you're in this mood!' He walked away to stand with his back to her, his hands thrust into his trouser pockets, looking broodingly out across the Downs.

She had wanted to go to him and apologise and say that she did not believe half of what she said, but a lurking fear that she might be right held her back. The incident had passed, but they had never bought the house. Lissa wondered if things would have turned out the same way if they had.

'Did you say something, girl?' Over the engine noise, Bill turned round in the front seat of the jeep and looked at her.

She must have been wondering out loud. 'No, nothing.' She shook her head, hiding her face in a flying pinwheel of silky, sunstreaked hair.

'That's okay, then.' But Bill still held her with a

look before he turned away.

The snow came early that year. Less than a month later, at the end of October, there was a light sprinkling, melting the moment it touched the ground and surfaces, but a warning of a long, hard winter just the same. The film crew, a nine-day wonder in the little town, had long since disappeared and there had been no further word from Grant. So much for his offer of a job! Like so much that had been said and done in the past, like all those publicity set-ups with his leading ladies that had given her so many sleepless nights, it had not been meant to be taken seriously. She wouldn't hear any more about working for Grant, any more than she was likely to get her divorce before the statutory waiting period was up—unless, of course, Grant decided he wanted his freedom.

'Lissa, is that you?' The spring-loaded storm door 'womphed' shut behind her against a bitterly cold November twilight and Wilma's voice floated from the living room on a cloud of scent from a bowl of out-of-season freesias on the hall table.

Lissa shut the heavy inside front door behind the storm door. 'Yes, it is.'

'You've got a visitor!'

Ramsay! Her first thought was that it must be Ramsay. After being delayed again and again, he had finally managed to get away from his oil deal negotiations in Mexico and he had come straight to her. Now she was safe. By coming home, Ramsay had made any decision for her. Not that she had ever had anything to decide. Ramsay knew about her situation. He was, if not happy, at least reconciled to waiting until her divorce came through. She hadn't mentioned Grant's suggestion in her letters because she knew Ramsay would never agree to her working for him for six minutes, let alone six months, to get her freedom.

Cheeks flushed from her short walk across the yard in the biting cold from the farm office to the house, she carried on across the hall into the living room with a confident spring in her step and came face to face with Grant.

He stood up as she came in, uncoiling himself slowly from the chair. 'Lissa!'

She was speechless, totally speechless. Shock, confusion about what he might have told Wilma to account for his visit, all combined to keep her silent. The Masseys knew she had been married—it had come out once in casual conversation—but with their customary tact they had never pursued the subject, reading her embarrassment when the fact had slipped out. What she didn't know, now—this minute—was if Wilma realised that the man standing watching her with an amused glint in her eyes was her husband.

The question remained unanswered as Wilma looked first at her and then at Grant, impressed with the presence of a film star in her house and her normally placid face alight with excitement. 'Mr. Ferries has just been telling me you've known each other for years,' she said equivocally. 'Isn't it a coincidence that he happened to be passing through and discovered you were here!'

'Yes, isn't it!' Lissa struggled for composure. 'Hallo, Grant,' she added, feeling Wilma expected it of her.

'Hallo, Lissa.' He took her hand, playing the secret game that only they knew. 'You're looking beautiful.'

'Thank you.' She stood there, her eyes locked in his, the glow of cold and anticipation that her unexpected visitor was Ramsay adding a luminous depth to her face and turning the white fur trim of her hood into a startling contrast for her coppery hair.

'I've suggested that Mr Ferries spend the night.' Wilma went on talking for them from her armchair beside the open log fire that supplemented the house's much more efficient forced-air heating system. 'He tells me he's going north tomorrow to check some film locations. Isn't it exciting?' She was a girl again. 'I've told him Bill or Clay can fly him.'

After he'd stayed the night. Lissa froze. She never wanted to spend the night in the same house with him again. 'I'm sure Grant—Mr Ferries—has his own plans,' she said swiftly.

'Grant will do—and from you, too, Mrs Massey.' Eyes that had suddenly become ice-hard micro-chips when Lissa had snatched her hand away softened as he turned to Wilma in her chair. Wife of Masseyville's leading citizen, rich, protected, and a member of one of the area's oldest families, even Wilma could not withstand the impact of the natural charm Grant possessed and exerted—when he chose. Watching Wilma blossom, Lissa knew that she was lost. He had planned this. Planned, for some reason of his own, that he should drop in as if by chance and then receive an invitation to stay overnight. Anything that she might say would be completely useless against the impression he had already made.

'How dare you weasel your way in here!' she hissed in an almost noiseless undertone.

An eyebrow lifted and he gave her an amused, sidelong look. 'How else was I going to persuade you that you should work for me?' he replied imperturbably.

CHAPTER FOUR

SHE had two choices, Lissa decided later when she was in her room changing for dinner. Either she could plead a sudden illness and not go down at all, or she could dress carefully and well and go down to dinner as if the unwelcome and totally shattering reappearance of her husband in her life was no more than a minor incident which she was now quite sophisticated and worldly-wise enough to take in her stride. How she carried it through would all depend on how good an actress she really was.

It was no good pretending the sight of him hadn't shaken her; more so, perhaps, than their first meeting in town. That had been coincidence; due to the sheer chance of a major production company choosing an out-of-the-way spot like Masseyville for their background location shots. But coming to the ranch had been deliberate. Grant had deliberately sought her out, asked questions and found out where she was for the purpose of persecuting her. He had decided that he would let her have her divorce, but first, for some devious reason of his own, he had decided she must pay a price. The only thing she had to be grateful for was that he apparently hadn't told Wilma about their true relationship.

She pulled the weight of her shoulder-length hair back from her face and studied herself in the mirror. The reflection of the lamplit room behind her with its old Colonial furniture and antique four-poster bed demanded elegance, and tonight she would be elegant. Her hair could be piled on top of her head and her green-flecked eyes with their naturally sooty lashes could speak for themselves in a setting of high cheekbones above a generously full, curved mouth. She had one dress, black, slashed front and back to a deep vee at the neckline and slit up the sides. Designed to be worn without a bra or slip, its effect, against a flawless skin without a trace of her earlier summer tan, would be one of the cool, poised assurance of a woman totally in control of her life—light years away from the teenager waiting for life to begin on a sunlit tropical beach.

As a further act of sheer bravado she took a

long, scented bath, instilling an expensive fragrance in her skin to move with her as she walked and, catching sight of herself in the mirror as she was about to leave her room, she added a touch of blush high on her cheekbones to give her already brilliant eyes a dangerous glitter. Now let Grant Ferries think he could ride roughshod over her!

Her high heels clicked on the polished wooden stairs as she went down to the library where drinks were always served before dinner and, at her entrance, two men turned. Bill Massey's eyes widened in obvious and open admiration; Grant didn't move, but then he smiled and a knowing glint appeared in his dark cobalt eyes.

'Come in, girl!' Bill's voice penetrated her sudden sense of defeat. It had taken Grant less than a second to see through her masquerade, and the dress that she had bought and had been keeping for Ramsay and their first night out together when he got back now seemed both showy and suggestive with its slashed neckline and its folds draping her long, slender legs.

Bill nodded towards the decanters. 'What will you have to drink?'

'Scotch, please ... on the rocks.' An eyebrow under its thin line of scar lifted in a silent, mocking question, but Lissa was past caring. Let Grant think what he liked. She needed more than her usual vermouth and lemon to get her through what promised to be a tense evening.

'One Scotch on the rocks!' Bill's stubby fingers entered her field of vision with a half full cut glass tumbler. 'Wilma should be down in a minute.' He went back to the decanter to refill his own glass, first raising it interrogatively in Grant's direction. 'Another?'

'No, thanks.' Grant's eyes had not moved; a man in a dinner jacket like his host but somehow far more powerful and far more dangerous with his lion-like mane of hair shining dully in the light from the scattered table lamps and his weight poised easily on the balls of his feet.

Strong feet with toes that gripped the sand: a subliminal picture of a younger man flashed across Lissa's brain. He was tired and drawn, standing against a background of a clear blue sea, and she felt her breast contract.

'Grant's been telling me he's offering you a job.' Bill still had his back to them as Lissa lowered her glass, trying not to choke on her first rash gulp of the strong liquor, but his remark did more than any drink to bring her back to the present and to her senses.

Grant! So it was Grant already. It had taken him less than the time it had taken her to change to win Bill's acceptance.

'And I've been telling him it's quite impossible,' she said coolly. 'I've got a job already.'

'There's no need for that to stop you.' Far from helping her, Bill was making matters worse. She already knew he had an almost paternal attitude towards her and now, it seemed, he was extending it to cover Grant. Although he was his only nephew, Ramsay, it seemed, was already taking second place. 'There won't be much for you to do here in the winter,' he went on. 'In fact, Wilma and I are thinking of going to Hawaii—at least until calving starts. Clay can deal with what needs to be done here—my foreman,' he added for Grant's benefit.

'So there you are,' Grant interjected smoothly, and only she could see him smile. 'That's the last obstacle gone.' He made it sound as if concern for the Masseys had been her sole reason for turning his job offer down.

'Sure—no hassle.' Bill went blithely on, apparently completely unaware of the undercurrents filling the quiet room, and also apparently completely forgetting about Ramsay, now due back any day, who would most certainly not be as happy about this seemingly golden opportunity that had presented itself. 'She can always come back here when you've finished with her—if you ever do!' He gave them both a knowing look; a handsome couple whom fate, with a little help from an old rancher, had thrown together.

And Wilma made matters worse. Lissa had no sooner got over seething about the characteristically high-handed manner in which both men seemed to think they could organise her life than Wilma, with the gentle voice and standards of an earlier age, was talking about Barbados and about the coincidence that had brought them together again, so much later, in this totally different world.

Coincidence, my foot! Lissa thought viciously. Their first meeting in Masseyville might have been

coincidence, but the situation tonight had been
totally manipulated by the man sitting opposite at
the dinner table while the housekeeper deftly served
sole meunière from a silver dish.

'Your parents are still on the island, aren't they?'
Wilma enquired.

'They certainly are,' Grant answered for her,
making it seem not only as if they were old friends
but as if her parents could not possibly have any
objection to their only daughter going off into the
wilds of Saskatchewan with such an obviously
attractive man.

As indeed her mother wouldn't, Lissa realised.
Once she had reluctantly accepted the fact of their
marriage, her mother had become Grant's greatest
fan. Even after their separation, her sympathies
had stayed with her son-in-law. Nothing Lissa
could say could change her loyalty, and the possibility of a reconciliation was in all her letters and a
recurring subject of conversation on Lissa's visits
home.

'They certainly are! In fact, I visited them only a
month or two ago.'

Lissa jerked her head up in surprise, brushing
the housekeeper's arm and almost sending a fillet
of sole with its buttery sauce sliding to the floor. 'I
didn't know you'd been there,' she said abruptly.

'But then there's a lot you don't know about
me, isn't there? It's how long since we've seen each
other? Two years?' His eyes held hers, taunting her,
it seemed, to reveal the secret of their marriage.

She backed away from the challenge. There

would be time enough to discuss their marriage later—through their lawyers.

'What's this movie of yours called?' To her everlasting gratitude, Bill changed the subject.

'*Obsession*.' Grant's eyes flicked over her and then left with a comet tail of blue. 'At least, that's its working title and I'd like to think that's what it'll still be called when it finally reaches the screen. It's about the obsession of one man to fight for an ideal, no matter what the odds and no matter if he destroys himself in the process.'

'It's about Louis Riel, isn't it?' Wilma's gentler voice put in.

'In general it's about Riel,' Grant agreed, 'and about the final Metis rebellion up north of here.' He nodded towards the north-facing windows and the desolate lands of muskeg and perma-frost hundreds of miles beyond the luxurious sweep of the long velvet curtains. 'But the story that appeals to me is only a small part of the actual plot. It's about a trapper—a man who's going to lose whichever way it goes. He's damned whether Riel wins or not. His obsession is that Riel should not be stopped.'

Lissa had to ask. 'Is that the part you're playing?'

'That's right.' He paused with his wineglass lifted and studied her across the rim. 'Norris Potter, the man you met in town the other week, will be artistic director. I'm executive producer and I shall also be playing the role of Massignac.'

Lissa knew very little about the Riel rebellion,

fought to establish an independent nation for the
mixed race descendants of the early French trappers and the Indians. It had taken place to the
north of where they were sitting around this highly
civilised table and it had failed. But what she had
known, instinctively, was that Grant would be
playing the part of the man with the obsession. It
was so in character. Grant never accepted anything
as a *fait accompli* until he had exhausted all possible means for change, and that was why she had
to stay on the alert. He might be determined, but
so was she, and the one thing she was determined
about was that she was not going to accept his
offer of a job, no matter what pressures he might
bring to bear.

And the pressure was on later that evening. Bill
and Wilma had gone to bed, intent, it seemed, on
doing all the wrong things from all the right
motives, and leaving them together. His tie off and
his dinner jacket unbuttoned, Grant leaned back
on the chesterfield in the living room, watching her
as she moved restlessly about, touching a soapstone
Eskimo sculpture here and a small jade dolphin on
one of the shelves in the alcove beside the curtained
window. How long would it be, she wondered,
before she could safely make her escape?

'Why don't you sit down?' In the shaded light,
his face had the look of an ancient Indian carving;
strong, remote, with a hint of enigma in the shadows around the eyes. 'No, not there.' He halted
her on her way to an easy chair. 'Here.' He looked
down at the chesterfield.

'Why should I?' Lissa said thoughtlessly.

He glanced up, stopping her in her tracks. 'I would have said why shouldn't you is more to the point? You were the one who said there was nothing left between us. Now you can prove it.'

'If you like.' She sat coldly, inches away from him.

'Have you thought about my offer?'

'Of a job? Yes. And I refuse it.'

'I'm surprised.' But far from looking taken aback, he even seemed amused. 'I had the impression you would do anything to get a divorce.'

For a second, the memory of the happy years intervened and she weakened. They had had a couch like this—no, not like this. It had had sagging springs and a faded cover—not this smooth brocade—but it had been in front of the gas fire in their first furnished flat in London when money had been as short as love had been plentiful and a touch, or even a look, had led to lovemaking which had left them exhausted and content in each other's arms.

She edged away from him to sit with her back pressed up against the padded arm. 'What point is there in discussing a divorce?'

'From my point of view, none,' he agreed calmly. 'In fact, the present situation suits me very well. There's no way I can think of that I'd actually be better off if we were divorced.' Morgan in his arms; a whole string of other beautiful women in his arms—and in his bed, if the gossipmongers and scandal sheets were to be believed. Why should he want his freedom when he could have everything he wanted without marriage? 'But you, I gather,' his lips twisted caustically, 'would prefer to have your freedom?'

'Yes.'

'Okay, then—tell me why.'

'So that I can remarry.' There—it was out! She had put it into words.

Grant turned his head and reached for the coffee on the table beside him, poured almost an hour ago and quite cold. 'And this time you're sure you're ready for marriage!' He spoke so softly she could barely hear him.

'I was ready at seventeen,' she answered, 'only I picked the wrong man.'

He looked back and the scar above his eyebrow puckered. 'Did you? So it's all over, then?'

'Between us?' She forced herself to remember the sight of him kissing Morgan; forced herself to sound contemptuous. 'Of course! What did you expect?'

There was a long, long pause. 'From you ... nothing.' He replaced his cup. 'What's he like?'

'Who?'

'This fiancé of yours.' He stopped. 'Or should I call him lover?'

She flushed. 'No, you should not!'

'Okay, then—this fiancé.' His lips twisted. 'What's he like?'

'He's in oil—an oil company executive.'

'I asked what he was like, not what he did.' He waited, but what could she tell him? That Ramsay was the complete antithesis of him. Dark where he was fair; heavily built where he was muscular; a man who assessed the odds before embarking on any enterprise. Unlike Grant, who had risked everything every time he had raced on one of the great Formula One tracks, Ramsay did not take chances. In asking her to consider marrying him, Ramsay must have assessed that the odds were on their side. With him, she would be safe. 'But if the job he does is more important than the man himself,' Grant went on as she sat silent, 'and if you're satisfied . . .' he shrugged.

'I am,' she answered furiously.

'Okay, then. Work for me for three months— not six, but three, and I'll give you your divorce. After all,' he toasted her over the rim of his empty coffee cup, 'what have you got to lose?'

'Nothing—but I don't give in to blackmail!'

'Who said anything about blackmail?' He sounded genuinely surprised. 'I'm offering you a clean, civilised divorce at the end of three months. There'll be no messiness, no loose ends to offend your precious Ramsay——' He must have heard Ramsay's name from Bill, Lissa thought in passing. She hadn't mentioned it. 'Just a businesslike arrangement.'

He watched her without moving, the intensity of his face belying the light tone of his voice. He was somehow manipulating her into a situation for his own ends, but she couldn't see what it was. It was most certainly not the job—he could get a secretary anywhere—perhaps it was some way of putting pressure on Morgan—for some reason or another. But she might as well stop wondering. She would never find out unless he chose to tell her, and meanwhile, there was Ramsay to consider. Ramsay had already mentioned that a sensational divorce could harm his career—Westerners were puritans, he had explained, or if not puritans, they were discreet—and a divorce, like anything concerning Grant, would be certain to be well publicised. But even for Ramsay's sake could she do this? Work for Grant? Be with him every day? There was no feeling left, she was sure of that, but it would still be an almost impossible strain.

'I'm surprised you're still hesitating,' he jibed at her. 'Surely you're not frightened you might succumb?'

'Of course not! You shouldn't believe in your own publicity!' Intent on hitting back, Lissa made the retort and instantly regretted it. A quirk of an eyebrow told her that he had registered the fact that she must have read the results of a public opinion poll putting him in a list of the ten most sexually attractive men in the world. Stung by his obvious amusement, she over-compensated and saw his slight smile change to anger. 'Nothing,' she said thickly, 'and I mean *nothing* you do could have the slightest effect on me!'

'In which case,' he said, 'this should leave you cold!' The sibilant menace of his whisper should have warned her, but she was totally unprepared for the force with which he reached out and pulled her to him, slipping the slashed bodice of her dress from her shoulders and holding her, naked to the waist, against his chest. Trapping her wildly flailing hands, he moved against her, relentlessly arousing in a slow, erotic motion as his mouth came down to force hers open and bend her head right back. She defied him with her eyes, willing them to stay wide open as his bored into them and staying rigid even when she felt the impatience of his fingers release her hair to fall in a silky cloak around her shoulders. This lovemaking had no love in it, she knew that, but the possession of his mouth and body brought back memories and she prayed his kiss would stop. Another second, and there would be nothing she could do to stop her eyelids closing, taking her into a world of whirling, swirling darkness in which there was no resistance; just the overpowering need he had always been able to arouse to have him make love to her.

'Congratulations.' Grant released her a moment before her willpower shattered, pushing her away and regarding her with eyes that could have been blue glass. 'You've made your point perfectly. Unfortunately, it rebounds on you. With such a total lack of interest, I see no reason in the world why you shouldn't work for me!'

Lissa rationalised it to herself a thousand times during an almost sleepless night, only thanking whichever God it was who had been watching over her that Grant had not guessed how close she had come to breaking point. Her terrifying response to his lovemaking must have been caused by memory, she frantically assured herself—it most certainly wasn't voluntary. Some deeply hidden physical chord had been struck and had responded, that was all. It was no more connected with feeling, real feeling, than the curtains draped across the window had any feeling for their rail.

By morning she was calmer. Almost calm enough to meet Grant on her way to the breakfast room and show no sign of noticing that he also remembered that his last sight of her the night before had been of her sitting bolt upright on the chesterfield with her hair around her shoulders and her arms crossed over her naked breasts. His eyes had burned her—branded had been a word she had not been able to get out of her head for a long time—before he had finally got slowly to his feet and left.

'You want coffee?' He spoke now with his back towards her and her briefly accelerated heart slowed down.

'Yes, please.' She sat and watched him pour two cups from the automatic coffee maker on the sideboard. The housekeeper came in as he turned and started to carry them towards her, bringing a silver-covered plate with ham and eggs for Grant and a rack of wholemeal toast for Lissa. 'Thanks, Mary.' She looked up at the housekeeper with a smile of relief. It was amazing how much less alarming he was when there was a third person in the room, even if, as far as Mary was concerned, there was never any response; just a quick look from black eyes in an impassive Indian face and a curt nod.

Grant sat down as Mary served him. He was

wearing a quilted, sleeveless vest over his open-necked shirt this morning and, with his mane of hair, he looked powerful and menacing as he took his place with his back to the wide double-glazed bow window.

'I've come to a decision about the job.' With Mary in the background relighting the spirit burner on the sideboard, Lissa took the plunge and lied. And it was a lie. She hadn't come to a decision, it had been forced on her. One other thing had dawned on her in the course of that long night had been that Grant's parting shot had been absolutely accurate. There was no reason why she shouldn't work for him—and every reason why she should.

If she persisted in refusing, it would be harder to deny any accusation he might wish to make that she was still, at heart, attracted to him. Irrelevant now—and totally untrue—it could still be worked into a big publicity angle when it came to getting her divorce. 'Star's Ex Still Carries Torch!' She could just see the headlines. She could also see Ramsay's face when he read them. She had been manipulated and out-manoeuvred, and although, with his back to the light, it was impossible to see his face, she was quite sure he was smiling when he looked across at her.

'I take it your answer's yes,' he said.

'I'll work for you—but nothing else!' Even against the light, his smile was obvious.

'Did I ever ask you to do anything else?' he said.

Later that morning they flew north, first to Batoche, the community that had been at the centre

of the Riel rebellion, and then farther north again
to the location Grant had picked in which to build
a complete film set of Batoche as it had been in the
mid-1880's. Bill piloted the plane and Lissa was
glad. If Clay had been with them, he would have
been in the pilot's seat with Bill beside him and
Grant next to her in the back. She might have been
forced to capitulate about the job, but she still
didn't think she could have stood a whole day so
close to him.

In Grant's opinion the job had obviously already
started and he shot a steady stream of notes in her
direction as they walked around the historic settlement. The film set was to be an exact replica, with
just one difference. Instead of the original con-
struction materials of sod and heavy, hand-hewn
logs, floated down the river and hauled in by ox
cart, the duplicate Batoche would be largely made
of plywood and man-made substitute, flown and
trucked in and then erected by the film crew's con-
struction people on the spot. In his first venture as
a producer, Grant was determined to have authenticity down to the smallest detail, and the rapid
clicking of his Nikon camera acted as an accom-
paniment to his quickfire notes as he shot roll after
roll of reference material.

Although Lissa would have died rather than
admit it, it was an effort to keep up, and her fingers
grew cramped and her mind spun as she filled page
after page with his concise, detailed instructions
and coped with the additional complication of
keeping her notebook steady as she walked along.

It was, she decided, just as impersonal and remote as if she really had been a secretary hired through an agency and starting work that morning.

It was a relief when Grant called a halt. It was also a relief when Bill pleaded hunger and put down at a little town on the flight home.

Sitting there at the formica table with the smell of coffee and french fries hanging in the air, she once more wondered how her husband could have guessed she would be so competent. As far as he knew, her typing had never progressed from the stage of a few letters pecked out on the old portable they had had in their London flat. It had been after she had left him that she had gone back to secretarial college to polish up the skills that were standing her in such good stead this morning.

But then, when had Grant ever questioned anything? Lissa asked herself as she shrugged her red, fur-trimmed parka on over her jeans and got ready to follow the two men out of the restaurant. He had always taken it for granted that he could demand and get the best.

She studied the confident set of his head and neck out of the corner of her eye when they were once more flying over the vast empty territory. With snow on the ground, the whole countryside was black and white with pine and leafless clumps of scrub poplar etching an irregular, monochromatic pattern. The only colour was the dull gold sheen of that confident, arrogantly set head, just inches in front of her.

The hair was longer now than it had been when

she had first met him in Masseyville; grown for the
part he was to play and already curling down over
the collar of his thick parka. She had only to reach
out and she could touch it—her fingers instinctively
moved forward, remembering what it was like to
be caught in that thick, crisp hair while their owner
was being kissed into a mindless sensuousness. She
drew back in her seat, shocked and horrified, and
the noise of the single-engined plane came crowding in on her. What was she thinking of? Her days
of lovemaking with Grant were over—permanently!

It was a relief when the day was also over and
they were flying south to Masseyville with a red
sun sinking way off beyond their right shoulders.
There were more people here; more to distract her
and give her reason to look away from him and
out of the window. There were far more farms and
settlements here than there had been in the empty
country north of Batoche, but that empty country
was where she would finally be going with Grant.

For Bill's benefit, Grant had talked about the
film unit he would be controlling in terms of an
army; a totally self-sufficient operation with its
own plane and radio operator for communication
with the outside world, and its own food and tem-
porary housing. The one exception to all this community living would be Lissa.

'She's there for my benefit,' he said to Bill with a
laugh, but it was his sidelong look that had made
her wonder how much of a joke his apparently half
joking comment really was.

The final heart-stopping moment of the day came when they were banking to come in downwind of the brilliant orange airsock at the Massey ranch. There was a car parked outside the house, one she recognised. Ramsay was back. While she had been thinking he was still in Mexico, without any warning, he was back.

He had come out of the house and was walking towards the landing strip by the time the plane had taxied to a halt and Grant—why did it have to be Grant?—was helping her out.

'Your fiancé?' A hand beneath each of her elbows, he looked down at her.

'Yes.' She was trembling.

The hands fell away. 'Then go to him,' he said dismissively.

'But don't you mind?'

'Mind?' He gave a snort of laughter, his breath white in the frosty air. 'Why should I mind? All I'm concerned about is that you'll be ready to start work in two weeks!'

CHAPTER FIVE

'RIGHT—cut!' The young assistant director's eyes flicked towards Norris Potter for confirmation. 'Okay, everyone, that's a wrap,' he said. 'We start again at daybreak in the morning!'

'Oh my God!' The leading man, a French

Canadian, playing the part of Louis Riel, groaned loudly in Lissa's direction as he went past. Perhaps he thought she had some influence with Grant, she thought wryly, but if he did, he was going to be disappointed.

One thing Grant hadn't mentioned when he was describing a location film unit to Bill Massey in terms of an army was that, as executive producer for this particular army, he intended to be its sole general. Norris might be its artistic director, but Grant was in charge. He had fought to find the financial backers, he had supervised every detail of the pre-production planning and, when the time came, he would take direction as an actor and play the small role that would add the lustre of his name to the film's box office appeal, but, for now, he was in overall command. Nobody had any influence with him and the punishing day after day, dawn to dusk schedule he had drawn up went ruthlessly on.

The only compensation was that the rushes, flown to the nearest small town each night and processed in a church hall that had been rented and turned into a specially equipped laboratory and private cinema proved that the effort was worthwhile. Even to Lissa, unused to piecing together short clips of film shot out of sequence and seeing them as a whole in her mind's eye, they had a quality well above the average run of historical films.

She made her frozen body straighten up from the folding stool on which she had been sitting with

her inevitable notebook in her hand ever since the
second session of filming had restarted that afternoon, and thanked her lucky stars for union re-
gulations. Even Grant couldn't override the union
rule that there had to be at least one break between
lunch and supper for the technicians, and so they
all benefited from at least a few warm minutes in
the catering hut. No one could work without the
electricians—even in bright winter sunlight, spots
and pups were needed to give highlights and kill
shadows—otherwise Grant would probably have
had all those not protected by the rules working
mercilessly on.

Lissa unclamped her gloved fingers from her
notebook and pushed it and her pencil into the
deep pouch pocket of her padded coat. She didn't
know where Grant was and she was too cold to
care. He insisted she be constantly with him when
they were filming, ready for any notes he might
shoot in her direction, but since the wrap had been
called, he seemed to have disappeared.

'You look frozen!' The small entourage that always accompanied Norris everywhere he went was
trailing past and a bundled-up figure at the tail
end of the line paused and glanced in her direction.

'I am!' Through the layers of woolly hat, scarf,
gloves, sheepskin coat and pants, Lissa recognised
Sandy, the continuity girl.

'Then come and have a drink.' Sandy nodded
towards Norris's trailer with its door opening and
closing on tempting light and warmth as crew
members piled in.

Lissa wavered. 'I shouldn't. I've got these notes to type up. Grant'll want them to go down on the plane tonight with the rushes.'

'There's plenty of time,' Sandy said persuasively. 'Come and warm up first and then we'll both go back to the Hen Coop together. I've got some work I've got to do as well.'

'Oh, all right,' Lissa scooped up her folding stool and propped it against the side of Norris's trailer. The prospect of going back to the Hen Coop alone wasn't too appealing.

It was the name that had been given to the trailer she and Sandy shared with the make-up girl and with the occasional actress coming up for a few days' filming. It would be warm, but it was isolated. Grant—Grant again!—had insisted that it be set slightly apart from the rest of their trailer village with its all-male inhabitants. The result was that it was closer to the black outlines of the pine trees marching down the hill behind the natural bowl of the location and every time she saw those trees, the overpowering frozen emptiness of their situation always struck her. There were wolves there and bears, but there was nothing else for miles, except the trailer village and the re-markably realistic film set it overlooked. Waiting for Sandy and going back with her was a much more attractive proposition than going back alone.

She clumped up the steps into Norris's trailer and added her padded coat and 'moonwalker' boots with their nylon outer covering and thick, insulated soles to the pile already taking up a great deal of the floor space just inside the door. As director, Norris, like Grant, rated a trailer of his own, but the number of people there already was filling it to overflowing and she was jostled by a young man with a glass in one hand and a bottle held safely above his head in the other. He introduced himself.

'Hi!' he said cheerfully. 'I'm Dave Hammond. Have a drink.' The warm air after a long day's filming in sub-zero weather and, Lissa judged, about half the contents of his glass, had had a very quick effect. She recognised him as the young assistant director who had called the wrap.

'What is it?' She squinted doubtfully up at the bottle.

'Rye.' He paused. 'I think! Anyway, who cares?' He hooked an empty glass from a shelf behind her and gaily filled it. 'Cheers!'

'Cheers!' She stared at it doubtfully. It was rye and it was strong. She considered her chances of emptying most of it away and substituting a soft mix. They were not good, she thought.

Meanwhile, the young man had been studying her. 'You're Lissa, aren't you? Grant's secretary. We don't see much of you.'

'Yes, that's right—and no, you don't!' Apart from Sandy, Lissa had deliberately had very little to do with the rest of the crew. Norris had somehow been persuaded to keep silent—she neither knew nor chose to know what pressure Grant had applied to stop him spreading the gossip that she

was his wife, and it was only occasionally that she
saw him looking from her to Grant and back again
in a highly speculative way—and she had decided
that staying slightly apart from everyone would be
the safest way in case something did, inadvertently,
slip out.

'Then I'd better make the most of my opportunity.' The young assistant was charming,
slightly tipsy and about twenty-two. Lissa started
to relax. 'Tell me about yourself,' he commanded
with an engaging grin.

'There's not much to tell.' She took another sip
of the undiluted liquor and smiled back.

'There must be!' he insisted. 'It's not every day
you get someone on the production team who, by
rights, looks as if she should be on the other side
of the camera. Those cheekbones! Those eyes!
Wow!' He juggled the bottle and the glass so that
he could make a camera angle with the thumbs
and forefingers of both hands and look through it
at her. 'Come with me to the Casbah and I can
make you a star!' His voice dropped half an octave
and he twitched his lip above his teeth.

'I think you ought to put that down.' For the
first time since Grant had flown her into the location, Lissa was beginning to enjoy herself. It was
foolish, it was silly but it was fun.

'What? Oh, sure.' He leaned across and wedged
the bottle on the shelf behind her head. 'But don't
think you're going to get out of it that easily!'
Having given her his Humphrey Bogart, he now
lapsed into what he obviously considered to be

German. He must have seen a lot of bad B-movies, Lissa thought. 'Ve haff vays of making you talk,' he said. 'Vair vere you born?'

'Canada.' Lissa entered into the spirit of the thing. 'Winnipeg, to be precise.'

'Then you're Canadian!' he sounded surprised. 'I thought you were a Brit.'

'I've lived in England, but not for long.' She glossed over that part of her life. 'I was brought up in Barbados.'

'In the West Indies?'

'Yes, that's right.'

'Then you are a citizen of the world, my dear!'

She wasn't sure if it was his Peter Lorre or his Orson Welles, what she did see as he put an arm around her shoulders was that his face froze and his eyes fixed, and stayed fixed, on a point somewhere behind her head.

'Lissa!' Grant's voice cut through the empty and somehow silent space and the boy began to back away. 'Are my notes typed?'

'No, I'm afraid they're not.' Why shouldn't she enjoy herself for once? Lissa deliberately kept her back to him.

'In that case,' a hand came out and equally deliberately took her glass, 'I suggest we go across to your trailer and get them done now. The plane's waiting. Now, Lissa!' he ordered as she didn't move.

How dared he order her about as if he owned her! She hated to give in, but she had no choice. Sensing his anger, the people around them backed away, leaving a cleared space to the doorway and her coat and boots. Lissa put them on, managing not to look at him once. The last thing she saw as she left the trailer was the white and rather frightened face of the boy she had been talking to.

The hand that gripped her elbow directly they were outside was most definitely not that of a boy.

'I can manage, thank you!' She tried to wrench free of the numbing pressure.

'I'm sure you can! In fact, I've just seen how well you do it!' The voice came sarcastically from just above her ear. 'But all I'm interested in now is getting you back to your trailer and getting my notes typed up.' He negotiated her across an icy patch and up the trailer steps.

Lissa fumbled with the latch. 'I'll bring them over to you when they're finished.'

'I'll wait.' He leaned across and pushed open the door. With him standing behind her, blocking her escape, she had just one place to go—inside.

They brought the cold in with them, but that wasn't entirely why her fingers were slow to get started, and she made several false attempts when she had taken off her coat and boots and sat down at the typewriter. It was more a feeling of selfconsciousness of Grant standing just inside the door. She could see him reflected in the shiny surface of the plastic flow chart thumbtacked to the wall at eye-level in front of her.

He hadn't taken off his parka, but he had unzipped it and he was, as usual, bare-necked and bare-headed in spite of the punishing cold outside.

The spacious trailer with its built-in bunks and separate office space suddenly seemed much smaller than it did even when Sandy and Jane, the make-up girl, were there. Lissa could also tell that he was angry—much angrier than the situation called for. He had some right to be annoyed, she acknowledged grudgingly as her fingers picked up speed and she transcribed her shorthand notes. She should have come back to the trailer and finished her work before going to Norris's; she knew the plane was always waiting on the frozen surface of the nearby lake to take advantage of the last of the day's light to make the flight back to civilisation with the cans of film from the day's shooting and the production notes for the laboratory technicians waiting in the converted church hall. But this was the first time she had failed to meet the enforced deadline, and surely she deserved some latitude.

'I've finished.' She stood up at last and stuffed the typewritten sheets into a brown envelope and gave them to him.

'Here.' In return, he handed her her coat.

'You want me to come with you?' She was surprised. She went to the weekly showing of the rushes, but Grant had never wanted her to fly down at night before to see the daily footage. Usually he went alone, or with Norris.

'No.' His response was just as chilling as the weather, but in spite of that, she was aware of a shiver of relief. With Norris, for once, apparently not going, flying out and back would mean hours alone with Grant. 'I want you to go across to the dining hall.' He cut across her protest that she would prefer to wait and go with Sandy. 'You're going *now*!' he emphasised. 'Get something to eat— it'll absorb the alcohol. I don't approve of my staff being hung over in the mornings!'

The implication made her furious. 'I had one drink . . . No, less than that.'

'Really?' He ostentatiously sniffed her breath. 'It certainly didn't look like it when you started typing!'

'I don't have to take this from you!' Lissa went to move away, but he stopped her with his hand on her shoulder.

'And I don't expect my secretary to get tipsy and start a flirtation with a junior member of the production team!'

'I was not tipsy and I was not flirting!' His second statement left her equally outraged.

'I see.' He regarded her with narrow eyes. 'But it seems you do expect some preferential treatment.'

'Preferential treatment?' She was totally non-plussed. 'I don't know what you mean.'

'Then let me explain,' he said icily. 'Everyone else on the unit appears to understand that work comes before enjoyment—you, it seems, are the one exception!'

She suddenly understood. Once, just once, she had gone for a drink before getting her notes typed up, and he was accusing her of this.

'What about Norris?' she flashed back, frustrated. 'And Sandy? They were both there . . . or hadn't you noticed?'

'What Norris does is none of your concern,' he answered. 'As for Sandy and that young man in whom you were taking such an interest, I'll be speaking to them later.' And without pulling any punches either, if the expression on his face was any guide. 'Nothing,' he emphasised, 'but nothing is going to be allowed to interfere with the completion of this film on time—if not ahead of budget and schedule.'

Certainly not the understandable temptation for a few crew members to relax and get warm before starting on the evening work of preparation that gave everyone a twelve or fourteen-hour day, Lissa added privately. Still, she had been half in the wrong. Delay—even the minor delay of a plane waiting for the rushes—cost money.

'I see,' she said ungraciously. 'I'm sorry.' If she had thought her apology was going to make any impression, she was disappointed. He studied her unblinkingly for a moment and then picked up her coat.

'Put it on,' he ordered.

'No!' She had apologised. What more did he want? 'I'll wait and go across to the dining hall with Sandy later.'

'You'll come now—with me,' he repeated. 'I don't like you being here alone.'

Any more than she had liked being alone in the flat in London all those times when he had been off on some glamorous location and she had been left with her imagination. She was wiser now about the glamour, but she was still angry. 'Why?' she retorted. 'Because you're worried in case I've got a bottle of rye hidden underneath the bed?'

'Maybe.' His face told her nothing. 'I just don't want you here alone.'

He walked her across to the prefabricated building that served as a dining hall, their footsteps scrunching across the frozen snow, and he left her at the doorway with a curt goodnight.

Minutes later, sitting at a trestle table with her main course and dessert in a pre-formed plastic tray, Lissa heard the sound of the plane taking off and taking him away.

Just as she would be flying out of the location and then driving on farther south to Masseyville at the end of that week, she kept reminding herself as the remaining days went past. Also, come that weekend, she would be a third of the way through her stint as Grant's production secretary; a third of the way through the commitment he had made a condition of her freedom. In two months, divorce proceedings would begin, with no messiness and no loose ends. He had promised her that, and she knew him well enough to know that he would keep his word. What she couldn't understand was why something she had once sought so eagerly seemed to have lost some of its appeal.

'Work for me for three months and prove there's nothing left!' That had been his argument and, of course, there was nothing left.

What they had once had had been killed by the long process of loneliness and jealousy when he had seemed to have time for everything—and everyone—but her. He had given everything to building his film career, wanting—almost needing—to be at the top, just as he had once been as a racing driver and would now be again as a film producer, she had no doubt. He had the drive, the ambition and the ruthlessness, but the other side of him was the tenderness and laughter they had once shared.

Physically powerful enough to crush her, his lovemaking had always been gentle as well as passionate—nothing like the angry assault on the couch at Masseyville which he seemed to have been able to forget completely.

But for her it had aroused so many memories, and sometimes, even now, weeks later, standing next to him with her mind free to wander as he dealt with one of the endless details of production not concerning her, she would find herself remembering the erotic stroke of his hand across her breasts and feel her skin pucker in an involuntary response. No one else had ever touched her quite like that—and no one ever would.

Ramsay had once obliquely suggested a weekend, but she had pretended to misunderstand the deeper meaning of his suggestion, and this weekend at the ranch the servants would be there as a restraint. Time enough to take Ramsay as her lover when they were married; meanwhile, he was everything she wanted—solid, dependable, unspectacularly handsome and, above all, conventional. There would be no long, unexplained absences with Ramsay, no stabs of terrifying jealousy when she picked up a magazine and saw his name linked romantically with one or other world-famous actress.

Maybe she would even be able to persuade him to take more of an interest in the Massey ranch. He was Bill's only heir, but the outdoor life did not appeal to him, and it saddened her, almost as much as Bill, to think that when he inherited he planned to sell.

But Ramsay was the man she was going to marry. Anything there had ever been with Grant was dead—lost in the past—and the following weekend, her first free one since this interminable testing time had started, she would be back at Masseyville with him.

When the two men had first met, Ramsay's hostility had been immediate and intuitive. He had stood beside the plane on the ranch landing strip with his head lowered on his thick shoulders like a bull about to charge, while Grant had watched him with that private glint of amusement that she knew so well. But it had been Ramsay who had backed down, muttering a few standard civilities when Bill Massey had introduced them and then taking Lissa's arm and hurrying her into the house.

She had deliberately swept her hair up that evening and worn the gold earrings Ramsay had given her to serve as an engagement ring until the way was cleared for their engagement to be formally announced. They fitted with his image of their future; solid and substantial, to be lived in a house somewhere in one of the more exclusive suburbs of Calgary, and she saw the glow of ownership light up his face when she walked into the library and he noticed them.

She also saw Grant's smile as, with some sixth sense, he seemed to guess their meaning, and she had gone a little crazy. She talked too much, she flirted, aware of Wilma's puzzled looks but unable to stop herself chattering continuously on.

'Don't you think you're taking this performance a little too far?' Grant had manoeuvred himself beside her on the long walk from the library to the dining room.

She defiantly tossed her head. 'Surely you're not jealous?'

He shrugged indifferently. 'Why should I be? If you choose to use Massey as a shield for your emotions, that's entirely your affair.'

Lissa was furious. 'What you're saying, in fact, is that I'm using Ramsay as a protection against you!'

'If you like to see it that way, yes,' he answered coolly.

There was no hint of where his feeling might lie, she noticed angrily. But then she knew that already. They were with Morgan or with one or other of the rest of the beautiful women with whom his name was constantly linked. Her anger reached flashpoint.

'Then let me set the record straight,' she blazed. 'Once this is over——' her incoherent gesture encompassed him, the house and the three months that lay ahead of her, 'it will give me a great deal of satisfaction never to see you again!'

But the interchange had sobered her, and she sat at the dinner table seeing Ramsay with new eyes. Was she really sure he was the man with whom she wanted to spend the rest of her life? Of course she was! To test her reactions, she deliberately let her eyes slide the length of the polished table and rest on Grant. His hair gleamed in the candlelight and his face was mobile and alive as he discussed some point with Wilma. The old familiar ache behind her breastbone stirred and she rationalised it angrily away. It was only natural that he should have some effect on her. No one ever forgot their first love, however disastrous it might turn out to be.

'And how long do you say you're going to work for him?' Ramsay started to question her immediately Grant and the Masseys had gone upstairs to bed, standing in front of the great fireplace in the library with his head lowered in his characteristically bull-like way.

'Three months.' It had been difficult enough to persuade him not to tell the Masseys about her relationship to Grant. Ramsay had to know—had known since the day he had first mentioned marriage and he had grudgingly accepted her reasons for not wanting to make the information common knowledge. A man like Grant drew publicity— Lissa had noticed one of the young reporters from the local paper at the front of the crowd around the location filming. What a scoop for a novice journalist to be able to report that, in choosing an obscure town on the prairies as a location, an internationally known film star had accidentally stumbled across his wife! Ramsay understood, and disliked, that sort of publicity.

'Three months, eh?' He considered the ultimatum over his brandy glass. 'I don't like it,' he added through pursed lips, 'but I guess there's nothing I can do.'

There was! He could have said to hell with the divorce. He could have insisted she go and live with him in Calgary so that they could fight the situation together until they won. That's what Grant would have done. But that wasn't Ramsay's way. He lived by the proprieties.

The crowning touch to a highly difficult evening had come when Ramsay had been kissing her goodnight.

'Excuse me!' The voice had come from the stairs and they had sprung apart.

Grant was standing half way down in a direct line with the open door of the library, and the brilliance of the overhead chandelier made it easy to read the cynical amusement etched in every line of his face.

'I'm sorry if I interrupted anything,' he drawled, 'but I couldn't sleep. I came down to get a book.'

CHAPTER SIX

'LISSA!' Ramsay's voice and the outline of his stocky figure against the open front door were the first things she heard and saw when she drove up to the ranch house late on the Friday evening of her first precious free weekend.

When she had gone filming, she had driven the Volkswagen to Rosglen, the little town where the laboratory and rushes theatre had been set up, and had garaged it there before she had flown farther north to the location. Coming back to the car earlier that evening had been like coming back to an old friend from a former life.

Ramsay must have been anxious to see her, she thought as she got wearily out of the front seat. To be there ahead of her, he must have left the office early—an almost unheard-of happening—and driven hard from Calgary.

'You're late. That fellow hasn't come back with you, has he?'

'No!' How nice it would have been if he had kissed her before he started asking questions. Grant was most certainly not with her. He was still back at the location, immersed in details for the next week's filming schedule. He had barely glanced up when she had opened the door of his trailer to say goodbye.

'Never mind, you're here now.' Ramsay's lips were moist and demanding. 'Come inside. I've had Mary leave some supper for you.' He left his arm possessively around her waist as he walked her into the house.

'I think I'm too tired to be hungry.' She followed his example, feeling his solidity underneath her arm.

'Darling, I've missed you.' He started to kiss her again the moment they were in the lighted hall.

'No, Ramsay, don't!' She pulled away. 'I've got to go upstairs and shower. There aren't too many home comforts on location!'

It was true that the bathing facilities on location were primitive and draughty, to say the least, but she still didn't know if it was an excuse or not. What she did know was that the minutes under a real hot shower, after so long without, were blissful. She also sensed that she would have to be careful. There had been an urgency about Ramsay's kisses that had never been there before and, apart from the servants, they were alone in the house.

The Masseys had gone to Hawaii leaving the house in the charge of their housekeeper and her squad of maids and the ranch with Clay, the cattle warmly housed in the great barns and the one or two hired hands kept on for the winter living with Clay in the bunkhouse in one corner of the windbreak.

Lissa went to the built-in closet in her room and looked through the clothes hanging there, choosing a soft beige velour jump suit, closing high up at the neck, and a pair of wedge-heeled mules. Her shoulder-length hair could be left to dry naturally—one of the advantages of natural waves—and, with a touch of lip gloss, she was ready. She was also more confident. There were, after all, people in the house. She went downstairs.

Ramsay was waiting for her in the living room with a Martini and a chicken salad sandwich with all the trimmings on a tray on the occasional table beside a chair. She sank back against the padded headrest and began to eat, revelling in the sensation of being clean and totally spoiled after the weeks of spartan living conditions.

'I'm not so sure if this is a good idea.' Ramsay was standing with his back to the fire watching her.

'What?' Lissa asked dreamily.

'This three-month arrangement you've been talked into.' The fire was giving his face a beefy glow and his lower lip was aggressively thrust forward.

She sat up slightly, on the alert. 'But why? You agreed.'

'I don't seem to remember having much choice,' he accused. 'It was all cut and dried by the time I came back from Mexico, as I remember.'

'But what alternative do we have?' She waited. Perhaps the weeks apart had made him think again about defying the conventions. Perhaps he really was going to suggest that they lived together or that they take the chance and fight what could be a highly publicised and sensational divorce. Grant, she was sure, would not give in gracefully, and the publicity was hardly likely to worry him. If anything, it was likely to add to his box office appeal as a hell-raiser with women.

She found herself sitting tensely in the chair. If Ramsay did suggest they live together, she was going to refuse, she realised suddenly.

'There's no alternative, I guess.' He backed down and she was conscious of a flutter of relief. 'But if that fellow tries anything . . .!' he finished on an empty threat.

'He hasn't,' she was quick to reassure him. 'And it doesn't look as if he's going to.'

That at least was true. Quite apart from having apparently forgotten those moments on the chesterfield in this very room when the searching pressure of his hands and mouth had come near to destroying the independent peace of mind it had taken her two years to achieve, Grant had, if anything, shown less interest in her than he had in anyone else on the production team. Aside, that was, from accusing her of neglecting her work!

He had obviously kept no memories to plague him. Memories of the happy times; the months and years when they had been so close that it had taken only a look to read each other's thoughts.

But that was over—dead and gone. Finished the day she had walked out on him. She forced herself to listen to what Ramsay was saying about his plans for the weekend.

'The Lewchuks are giving a housewarming tomorrow night. I told them we'd drive over, if you're not too tired.' He looked at her hopefully.

'No, that's fine.' In fact, it was far from fine. She had been looking forward to a long, lazy weekend before she had to make the drive north to catch the plane back to the location on Sunday evening. Now, it seemed, she was going to have the long drive across the Alberta border into Calgary and back and, on top of that, the strain of a formal party with people she didn't know. But Bud Lewchuk was president of the oil company for which Ramsay worked and Ramsay wouldn't want to miss an opportunity to make his mark.

She was incredibly depressed that night, shifting restlessly around in the big fourposter bed long before she could get to sleep. And yet she should have fallen asleep instantly. It was the first time she had slept in a proper bed rather than her narrow bunk in the Hen Coop for more than three weeks. The chicken salad sandwich had been a meal rather than just a snack and, almost as if she had had a premonition, she had had a brandy with her coffee afterwards, but still she couldn't get to sleep.

She must be missing the companionable sound of Sandy snoring, she thought, turning over for the umpteenth time. The continuity girl would deny the fact to the death, but when she settled into a really deep sleep, she ground her teeth and the trailer almost rocked to a series of deep, loud snores.

Lucky Sandy! She would probably be sleeping

now—and so would Grant. Lissa turned over irrit-
ably. It was her weekend off and she had promised
herself she wouldn't think of him; a promise she
had already broken more than once already. But
Grant was on location three hundred miles away
and it was Ramsay who was sleeping in one of the
bedrooms farther along the corridor; saying goodnight with a bad grace, one eye on the bed behind
her and wanting more than one quick kiss when
she had gently but firmly eased him back and
closed her bedroom door.

'I can't get over how fabulous you look!' Ramsay's
eyes slid constantly towards her on the long drive
to Calgary late the following afternoon.

'Thank you.' Lissa turned her head towards the
flat white landscape passing outside the heated
window of the Jaguar with little indication of their
speed. Moose Jaw and Swift Current were behind
them and they had crossed the provincial border
into Alberta from Saskatchewan. Now there was
just Medicine Hat and the long haul across what
Lissa privately called the empty deadlands before
they saw Calgary, a journey of several hundred
miles—but then, by Canadian standards, driving
miles—even if you counted them in hundreds and
especially if you were driving them to an important
party—was commonplace.

It had seemed ridiculous putting on full evening
dress so early in the afternoon, particularly when
she was still not over the effects of staying awake
until nearly five and then sleeping heavily until

almost noon—something that had pleased neither Ramsay nor the Masseys' housekeeper. Mary liked meals served at the proper times, not breakfast waiting until nearly lunchtime, and Ramsay had made no secret of the fact that he had not appreciated having to spend the morning on his own. So Lissa had taken trouble with how she looked, pushing aside the slinky black dress which she had been keeping for just such an occasion and choosing another in a subtle shade of green, just deliberately short of a complete match with her eyes.

She doubted if she would ever wear that black dress again. It had been bought for Ramsay, but Grant had irrevocably put his stamp on it.

She had no such choice, though, when it came to choosing a coat to wear. The Lewchuks, Ramsay had informed her with a great deal of pride, were multi-millionaires and walking up to their front door in a Hudson Bay parka of thick red wool with a fur-trimmed hood or in the near ankle-length quilted coat she wore for filming most certainly would not do. All she had was the dark Russian sable Grant had given her for their last anniversary together. Putting it on had been like going back into his arms.

'Now, you remember what I've told you about the Lewchuks?' Ramsay asked as they topped a slight rise and the lights of Calgary sparkled in the great natural bowl ahead of them.

'Yes, I remember.' She should: he had gone through it a dozen times. 'Bud is your boss. Irma's his wife and they have three children, all of whom are quite brilliant and beautiful.'

'Right!' The sarcasm passed him by. 'But Bud and Irma are a bit straitlaced, so I don't think we should mention the ... well,' he shrugged, 'the arrangement between us, but you can talk about Ferries if you like.'

'What?' She could hardly believe her ears. Ramsay was making their understanding sound like an affair, but he didn't seem to mind her telling everyone she was already married.

'I don't mean tell them you're still married to the guy,' he explained hastily, 'but you might like to mention that you work for him. Irma would like that. She's into movies and that sort of thing. Say!' he was suddenly more animated than she had seen him the whole day. 'Perhaps you could get her invited up to the location? But no,' he added more soberly as he turned into the beginning of what was obviously a private road and a torch-swinging guard stepped forward to check their licence plate and wave them through, 'I guess Irma wouldn't want to travel all that way. But just let on a bit about his private life. There's no need to tell her how you know.'

His degree of insensitivity astounded her. She had known he could be single-minded when it came to the advancement of his career, but not to the extent of benefiting from the reflected glory of a man he had earlier not been able to say enough against.

'I'll try!'

For an instant something in her voice must have

touched him and he looked at her curiously as they drew up outside a large white-painted house. 'Thanks, Lissa,' he said softly. 'And don't worry, it'll all come out okay in the end.' He leaned across and clumsily brushed her mouth. 'And have I told you, you look fabulous!'

With her arm through his and introduced by name but with her status left discreetly unexplained, Lissa could understand why he had been so nervous. Once inside the Lewchuks' house, it was a hard, fast, wheeling and dealing atmosphere; the men with rapid twanging voices and calculator eyes and the women covered in jewellery—real jewellery. They had been invited to a housewarming and they had come to score points.

'Joan—honey!' Minutes later, Irma Lewchuk was prying Lissa away from Ramsay and taking her across to the women grouped on one side of the room. 'Joan!' she tapped a woman of about her own age peremptorily on the arm. 'You must meet Lissa. She's working for Grant Ferries—you know, honey, the sexy movie star!'

From that moment on, no one wanted to talk to her about anything except Grant. What he was really like; how he behaved off-screen, even what he ate for breakfast. It was true! One of the women really wanted to know that, and one of them, presumably less 'straitlaced' than the rest, even wanted to know if he had ever tried to make love to her.

Perhaps that was why, when they finally got back to the ranch in the early hours of the morning after an interminable drive, Lissa didn't ease

Ramsay quite so firmly away from her bedroom door. More than anything else, she wanted to expunge all thought of Grant; overlay it with something else so that her first thought wouldn't be of him when she woke up in the morning. Sensing her changed mood, Ramsay slid his hands slowly down her back between her dress and the Russian sable coat.

'Darling!' She stopped thinking about the future as he pulled her to him, but his breath was stale and smoke-filled, so different from the clean astringency of Grant's, and his kiss was suffocating.

Why couldn't she stop thinking about Grant? She moved her head to breathe and Ramsay's lips slid down her neck towards her breasts. Even now she was comparing them. Why couldn't she relax and let go?

Her coat dropped from her shoulders to the floor, slipping sensuously along her back and legs, and the memories of Grant increased. Downstairs, a telephone began to ring.

'Ramsay, I can't!' She put her hands against his chest and pushed him away, and his face came up, slack and flushed, filled at first with frustration and then with angry bitterness.

'Why not?' he demanded. 'A moment ago, everything was telling me you could!'

'I don't know why!' she said desperately.

The telephone had stopped. With part of her mind working independently, she realised it was already getting light. Mary and the maids must be up and about and one of them must have answered the telephone.

'It's him, isn't it?' He refused to use Grant's name. 'Don't think I haven't noticed the change in you since you got back from that damned filming. My God!' the thought struck him. 'And Bud was so taken with you that I mentioned we were thinking of getting married!'

'But we are!' Lissa clung to it. 'In a few months I'll be free.'

'Will you?' He looked at her quite coldly. 'I doubt it. You might be getting your divorce, but I wonder now if you're ever going to get *him* out of your system. I warn you, Lissa, I don't take another man's leftovers. One day you're going to have to make a choice.' He stood there, head lowered, waiting for her reaction and then, with a hiss of exasperation, he turned and walked away.

Through the slamming of his door, Lissa slowly bent and picked up the symbol of her marriage, lying in soft silky folds around her feet, and rubbed the dark fur against her cheek. Grant might not be there in person, but he was still doing an excellent job of ruining her life a second time.

Ramsay was already downstairs when she went down the following morning, the business sections of the Sunday newspapers scattered on the floor around him in the living room.

'You want breakfast?' The housekeeper had followed her silently into the room.

'No, thanks, Mary.' Lissa forced a smile even

though the fatigue and depression that had hung
around her like a cloak was even worse now after
the scene with Ramsay. 'If you've got coffee going,
I'll have a cup. Otherwise, I'll just wait for lunch.'
She was determined not to antagonise Mary just
as she was determined to put things right with
Ramsay. She had been a fool the previous night.
With Ramsay she was safe.

'What about him? Will he be staying for lunch?'
Mary enquired stolidly.

Lissa didn't understand. 'Ramsay? Of course.'
She turned to him, enquiring, 'You're staying,
aren't you, darling?'

Mary answered. 'Not him—the other one. The
one in the library.'

'The other one? Who? Who does she mean?'
Lissa looked back at Ramsay as Mary stood
impassively in the doorway.

He stood up and a chill struck her. 'Ferries,' he
said coldly. 'He flew down first thing this morning.
He wants you to go back with him. Will you go?'

Her future rested on her answer. 'Darling,' she
went to him, but it was like touching stone.
'Darling, be reasonable! I work for him, that's all.'

He studied her levelly. 'Is it?' he asked. 'I told
you last night you were going to have to make a
choice. Call me when you have—if it's not too late!'
With more dignity than he had ever had before, he
walked past her and through the door without another word.

Ignoring Mary, Lissa hurried to the library and
flung open the door. 'How dare you do this to

me!' The impetus of her anger had got her there but, at her first sight of him, she stopped: aware of the sudden jolt in her stomach and fighting for control.

'Do what to you?' He was smiling, completely unconcerned, his teeth glinting in the beard he was growing for the part he was to play and which had suddenly taken shape and form in the days since she had seen him. In the eminently civilised surroundings of the Masseys' library, he looked powerful and untamed; a man quite capable of the obsession of the role he was to act.

'Ruin my life!' The moment she had her breath in check she flung it at him.

'You flatter me!' He turned and replaced the book he had been reading back on the shelf, the delicate way he handled it belying the overall impression of strength. His shoulders moved the denim shirt and his waist and hips were slim and hard under the broad leather belt and the white chino pants. 'I didn't think I had so much influence!' He was still smiling when he turned back, but his eyes were hard and brilliant.

'You don't!' A car started up outside and backed across the yard; Ramsay must be leaving.

'Then why are you so upset?' An eyebrow lifted, mocking her: he had heard the car as well. 'I'm sure if you run after him you can persuade him to come back.'

'Ramsay has nothing to do with this!' She refused to give him that satisfaction.

'Really?' he smiled.

'Yes, really.' Now she was angry, really angry. 'What I want to know is why you're persecuting me!'

'Persecuting you? My dear Lissa,' his voice was light, amused: he was acting, playing a game, 'I'm not persecuting you. I need you on location, there's been a change of schedule and I want you to fly back with me. I called earlier. Didn't you get a message?'

No, she hadn't got a message, but she had heard the telephone. Earlier, much earlier, when she had been arguing with Ramsay. 'Then I'm afraid you've had a wasted journey,' she said icily. 'I intend to drive back and leave my car at Rosglen.'

'And I'm telling you that you'll fly back with me!' There was no pretence of play-acting now. The smile had gone and there was a harsh rasp in his voice. For a second, just a second, Lissa had the impression of something more behind his arrival than a crisis at the location. But that was impossible. Just as impossible as her hope when she had come downstairs that morning that she could work out at least some understanding and reconciliation with Ramsay before the weekend ended. Grant was going on, making it quite clear that his badly-timed arrival had nothing to do with any personal motive. 'As I said, there's been a change in the shooting schedule and it means a lot of extra work for everyone. If you drive back, you won't be able to get the plane out to the location until tomorrow morning. I need you there to do some work tonight.'

'But it's my weekend off, or had you forgotten that?'

'There are no weekends off when it comes to meeting a production deadline,' he informed her flatly. 'I warned you of that when you took the job.'

'Which you gave me no alternative but to take, as I remember!' She saw his face harden and went rashly on. 'Perhaps you should also have warned me that you consider paying a salary gives you the right to own your employees body and soul! Excuse me,' she finished, 'I have to go and get my things and tell Mary there'll be no one here for lunch.'

'Lissa!' His voice stopped her halfway through the door, reaching out to envelop her and stir the hairs on the nape of her neck. 'Don't tempt me to do something that we'll both regret!'

Her last sight of him as she ran up the stairs was of him standing watching her with his back against the light.

She had expected the film unit's pilot to be with the plane, but when they got out to the landing strip, she realised Grant was alone. He must have brought it down himself, she thought. His ideas about everyone being totally subservient to the demands of the shooting schedule obviously did not apply to some members of the crew. The pilot, at least, was left to have his weekends undisturbed.

She didn't pursue the subject. Instead she sat there, silently watching the confident hands lift the plane up off the landing strip and leave the ranch behind. The climb finished, they settled into the steady drone that would eat the miles as they flew over the snowbound countryside until they reached the frozen lake that served as the location's landing strip. As dusk came on, so the lights appeared below; an amazing number for country that seemed empty in daylight and only at night gave any indication of its population. Farms with house and yard lights, small villages clustered about their brilliantly lit main streets and, beyond it all, the great natural phenomenon of the Northern Lights, flickering and dancing on the horizon like some great city permanently out of reach.

The cabin was warm and she was sufficiently at home with the sensation of flying in a small plane to relax. Grant, it seemed, was concentrating totally on bearings and airspeed, and she risked a glance. It hardly seemed possible he was still her husband. She tried to look at him objectively, seeing him for the first time, but the stirring round her heart was that of the young girl she had been when they had met so long before on a sunwashed tropical beach. Would she ever get over it? she wondered. Ramsay was everything she wanted, she was convinced of that. Solid, dependable, four-square; her mother would totally approve of Ramsay as a son-in-law. At least, she would have done if she hadn't already met Grant first.

Besides, she had lost Ramsay. No, she hadn't. Her mind flip-flopped. Once this interminable three-month testing period was over, she could still go to him and put things right. She had been a fool not to make the choice last night. Standing in her bedroom doorway, it would have been so easy to tell him that she loved him and hope that time would make it a reality.

The plane droned on and she drifted, two almost sleepless nights sending her in a crazy chase through a maze in which Ramsay's voice and Grant's were continually calling her, forcing her to choose.

'Lissa, you'd better tighten up your seat-belt.' Grant's voice, real and totally without emotion, brought her up through layers of drowsiness into a world of suffocating dark. She could see his profile outlined in the glow from the instrument panel, but beyond that, where the spotlight and navigation lights should have been, there was nothing except a thick grey wall.

'Why?' Although she questioned, she automatically obeyed him, pulling the canvas belt through the metal clip.

'The cloud's closed in. We should be somewhere near Rosglen and I'm going to try and make a landing. It's too dangerous to fly on to the location tonight.'

He had brought her alive and now they were going to die together. The thought was melodramatic but strangely calming. It was inevitable that she should be with him. He was the love that was never-ending, no matter what—or who—came between them. She looked at him, holding the bucking plane as they went through an updraught in the thick cloud ceiling. Emotion made it difficult to speak.

'Darling, I love you,' she said chokily.

Had he heard her or not? There was no way of telling from his impassive face as the ground came rushing up at them out of the murk and they touched down, lifted, hung for an agonising second and then settled safely on a strip of frozen summer fallow.

Lights were going on outside a nearby farmhouse and people were rushing towards them across the field. Grant taxied to a halt and killed the prop.

'Are you okay?' His question was almost lost as people reached them, opening doors and holding up arms to help them out.

'Yes, I'm fine.' She called the answer back, aware of looks and glances as eyes turned towards him and their owners realised who he was, but most of all aware of the searching depth of expression on Grant's face as he looked across at her.

The northern cold was biting after Masseyville, but it wasn't cold that numbed Lissa's brain and kept her sitting silently long after the farmer and his two sons had taken them into a warm farm kitchen.

'Do you think he'd think me a fool if I asked him for his autograph?'

'What?' Lissa came to with a start. The woman of the house was glancing first at the blank page of a homework book on the table and then longingly across at Grant. Even in the far north of the prairies, he was recognised. 'Oh, no, I'm sure he wouldn't.' She tried a smile and it must have

worked, because the woman picked up the book
and went across to where Grant was standing with
her husband and the book's teenage owner.

Would he think she was a fool if she went across
and asked—not for his autograph but if she had
imagined those last few seconds in the plane? She
studied him: huge in his beard and quilted parka,
dwarfing even the substantial bulk of the farmer as
he smilingly signed his name.

Surely she hadn't been mistaken. Not even the
passage of the years and the beard could change
some things. It was warm beside the kitchen stove,
but she began to shiver. For a second, in spite of
the beard and in spite of the strain of bringing the
plane safely in to land, there had been love in the
face that had been turned towards her. The sort of
love that had been written there on a perfect tropical morning when a girl of seventeen had looked
up at the man who had just become her husband.

'If I can use your phone, then, we'll be on our
way.' Grant's voice cut above the rest.

'But you won't get that plane out of here
tonight,' the farmer objected.

'Maybe not, but I can get a message through to
my pilot. He can pick it up in the morning and my
secretary and I——' Grant stopped his explana-
tion to glance in her direction, 'can spend the night
in a hotel.'

'But you can both stay here.' She might be talking about both of them, but the farmer's wife only
had eyes for Grant as she anxiously made plans to
keep him there a little longer. 'We've got the room.

The kids can double up and . . .'

'It's kind of you,' Grant gave her a smile that, for years, would make her feel a little younger and a little more desirable whenever she remembered it, 'but we have to make an early start in the morning—especially early now that we've been held up—and it'll be easier if we do it from Rosglen.'

'I'll drive you in, then,' the farmer insisted and, sitting between him and Grant on the front bench seat, there was no chance to talk as the half-ton truck followed the tunnel of its headlights along the empty roads. All Lissa could do was relive those last few seconds in the plane over and over again in her mind.

She had told him that she loved him. The words had been wrenched out by fear; not fear of dying but of dying before she had the chance to tell him what he still meant to her. What she had no way of knowing was if he had heard over the throttled-back pitch of the engine and, but for that fleeting look, gone almost as soon as it had appeared, she could once more have denied the truth even to herself. But now it was too late. She loved him and she had always loved him, even when she had been fighting for her divorce—perhaps most of all when she had been doing that. The one thing she didn't know was if he still loved her in return.

'It's the only hotel in town open this time of year.' Their driver stopped the half-ton in a lit main street and looked doubtfully across at a building with a flat, stepped façade that probably hadn't seen a lick of paint or an alteration since the day it had been built. 'Are you sure you'll be okay?' he said even more doubtfully.

'We'll be fine.' It was cold as Grant shifted the pressure of his body away from Lissa along the seat. His hand on the door handle, he looked across her. 'Perhaps you and your family would let me arrange for you to be flown up to the location one day as my guests?'

'Sure would!' Underneath the flaps of his fur hat, the man beamed.

'I'll have my secretary arrange it, then.' He opened the truck door. 'Lissa—are you coming?' There was nothing as he got out and stood beside the open door and waited for her. No sign of warmth or a special relationship; just a man waiting for his secretary.

'Yes, of course.' She forced a smile for the farmer sitting beside her. 'Thank you very much,' she said, 'and thank your wife. I'll call you about coming up to see us.'

Grant led the way into the hotel vestibule. It was surprisingly dark after the sodium lights outside and the man who eventually pushed open the swing door behind the desk must have been the one person in northern Saskatchewan not to recognise his famous guest.

'Are you hungry?' Grant scribbled an indecipherable name in the register and glanced across at her.

'No.' She wasn't hungry. She was tired and confused and there was a great void in her stomach every time she looked at him, but the emptiness had nothing to do with that sort of hunger.

The desk clerk settled the matter. 'Dining room's closed,' he said through the noise coming from the bar behind him. 'We can do you sandwiches.' He slapped two keys with metal tags down on the counter. 'Rooms are at the top of the stairs—fourteen and fifteen.'

'Sandwiches, then,' Grant ordered. 'Beef if you have them. And a bottle of rye.'

'The boss don't allow liquor in the rooms,' the clerk said stolidly.

Lissa saw Grant's temper rise. He pulled a twenty-dollar bill out of his pocket and put it on the counter. 'See what you can do,' he said abruptly. 'And I'll want to use your phone.' A man came out of the bar and eyed Lissa up and down: a woman was presumably a rarity in this type of hotel. 'You go on up,' Grant ordered.

She wondered who he had to call. Not the pilot, that he had already done, and not the location: calling the location was a complicated process that meant getting through on the radio. But whoever it was, it did not take long. She heard him go past her door shortly before the sandwiches came together, surprisingly, with a pot of amazingly good coffee. The rye, if any, presumably went next door. There was certainly a conversation: the desk clerk's monosyllabic monotone mixed with Grant's voice.

Her room was basic but comfortable—someone obviously cared about the condition of the hotel upstairs—with a high, old-fashioned bed and a huge mahogany wardrobe, big enough to house a family. Not that she would be needing it. Her bag, with her clothes, was still in the plane. She had just what she stood up in to take her through to the pre-dawn call that was to get them to the airstrip ready for the flight to the location.

And that pre-dawn call meant that she should get to bed and get some sleep, but the thought of Grant next door, separated by just a few inches of lath and plaster, kept her prowling restlessly around the room. She could hear him, too, apparently just as restless as she was herself, making the boards creak as he moved.

She must have been mistaken. Everything that had happened since told her that the deeply searching expression she had seen on his face just after the plane had landed must have been a figment of her imagination.

Two rooms—not one. Surely if he had really heard her tell him that she loved him, he would have booked one room. She was his wife and she knew him well enough to know that he would have overridden any protest on her part and ignored any assumption the desk clerk might have made. Instead, he had asked for two rooms, one for himself and one for his secretary.

Her clothes might be in the plane, but her notebook and pencil were in the pocket of her coat. She went and got them out. Grant had said he had come down to the ranch because there was work to do, but was that the only reason? She had to know—she must know—and she had one excuse for finding out.

Quickly, before she could change her mind or think through all the implications of what she was about to do, she walked to her door, opened it and went and knocked on his.

'Come in!' He was sitting in the one armchair; like her, fully dressed. His head under the mane of hair lifted and he looked at her, standing nervously in the doorway, as if surprised to find her really there. She ran her tongue across her lips; it was difficult to speak. Grant filled the silence for her. 'Do you want a drink?' He nodded to the unopened bottle and untouched glass on the table beside his chair.

'No.' She swallowed nervously. 'You said you had some notes.' She held out her book: a small defence against the sight of him.

'Notes?' For an instant he seemed puzzled, then he recovered. 'Aren't you too tired?' he mocked. 'I didn't know I'd hired the perfect secretary!'

The trance in which she was moving broke and she was angry; angrier than she had ever been in her life. 'How dare you say that to me?' she blazed on the thick edge of incoherence. 'There aren't any notes, are there? You've tricked me into this! You came down to Masseyville deliberately to ruin my weekend!'

He ignored the accusation. 'I think you'd better close the door. The entire hotel will hear you.'

'I don't care if they hear me . . .!'

'But I do.' With a speed that shouldn't have been possible, Grant uncoiled himself from the chair and strode across the room towards her, shutting the door and trapping her in the cage of his arms as he leaned against it. 'And now,' he tested her with his face inches above hers, 'tell me that you only came here to take notes! You're accusing me of trickery. Let's see how honest your motives were, shall we?'

He pushed her hair aside to brush the lobe of her ear with his lips, a well-remembered prelude to their lovemaking in the past, and set all her pulse spots throbbing. She fought to stand impassive but, in spite of all her will, her body curved, bringing her close against him, thigh touching thigh, breast against breast, and the pitiful protection of her notebook and pencil went clattering to the floor.

'It's two years, Lissa,' he said in a soft whisper. 'Two years since I made love to you. Do you remember?' He slid his hands across her shoulders, melting her blouse away. 'I think you do.'

Oh, yes, she remembered. She tried to resist, but memory was too powerful. Was it really two years since his hands had last slipped down her back like this, releasing the small clasp that hindered them and then moving on along the curve of her spine to mould her to him. She raised her arms, conscious of the weight of her freed breasts against his chest, and linked them round his neck. It couldn't be two years, it must be yesterday, otherwise how could she respond so naturally to a kiss that leaped and flickered on her mouth, and why did it seem no more than hours since she had last felt him lift her and, with a harsh exhalation somewhere between a sigh and a groan, carry her towards the bed? Feeling the strong beat of his heart against her own, she knew she had come home.

CHAPTER SEVEN

WHEN she woke the following morning, it was as it had always been—Grant's arm fitting easily around her shoulders and his hand cupping her breast. He was asleep and it was dark, but not so dark in the light coming from the street lamp through the curtained window that she couldn't see him. Careful not to wake him, she raised her head and studied him as she had done so many times before.

The beard made him a stranger, but the familiar planes and hollows of his face were there, with the sweep of eyelashes against his cheek giving him a vulnerability that would vanish the moment he awoke. Lissa's heart contracted and she slid her thigh gently along his, revelling in the special silkiness lovemaking always gave her skin, but for all her care, her slight movement must have penetrated the layers of his sleep: the arm around her tightened and he shifted his hand to cup her breast more closely. She held her breath but, with a deep sigh of contentment, he settled back to sleep again.

She had never loved him more than at that moment and, at that moment, nothing seemed impossible, not even the possibility that they could start again. Ramsay, everything that had happened in the past two years, had vanished in the course of that short night. And she had changed. She knew she had.

She was no longer the girl who had rushed out of their London flat in a fit of jealous anger. The two years since had given her a depth and a maturity that she had not then possesed. Always sheltered, always protected, first by her parents and then by Grant as she was, running away from her marriage had been the first consciously independent decision of her life. And it had been a wrong decision, she knew that now. If she had been honest, she would have acknowledged how much she had regretted it during those two long, hard years and how many times a false pride had stopped her going back. But at least that pride had given her one advantage. It had given her the time she needed to grow as a woman and now she knew she could encompass the demands of his career. The publicity, the long periods apart, all these would be bearable now that she knew she had his love.

But—her heart missed a beat and she felt cold in spite of the warmth of his body next to hers and the thick, downfilled duvet on the bed—did she still have his love? Not once during the long hours of lovemaking, with their bodies remembering without the need for words, had he told her that he loved her.

Her heart picked up its rhythm and he stirred, his eyelashes fluttering, and then coming instantly awake. For a moment he looked at her as if surprised to find her there and then he smiled.

'I thought you were a dream.' He spoke through the soft brushing of their lips, his shoulders hard and powerful in the dim light and the trace of his hand along the contour of her thigh driving out everything except a rising, all-consuming need for him.

The sound of footsteps and a sudden hammering on the adjoining room came only dimly through the prelude of their early morning lovemaking, but the sense of loss was real enough as Grant lifted his head and the hammering was repeated at their door.

'You awake in there?' Lissa recognised the grudging voice of the desk clerk who had signed them in the previous night. 'You wanted to be called at five-thirty! There ain't no reply next door, though!'

'Ssh!' Grant placed a finger gently on her lips and gave a wicked grin. 'It's okay,' he called, 'I'll let her know. And get a cab for me, will you? To the airstrip.'

'It ain't likely he'll want to go so early.'

Grant stiffened. 'Just get him, will you?'

The footsteps went away, clumping down the stairs. It was dark and the only light was the glow of the street lamp coming through the curtained window, but the day had begun.

'I don't want to go.' Lissa looked up at him.

'We've no choice.' There was a second's tenderness and then he had gone, pulling back the coverlets in one swift motion. 'Come on, get showered. The plane will be waiting. We've got work to do!'

Could this really be the man who had spent the night making love to her? Later, in the plane, flying over miles of forest just becoming visible in the increasing light, Lissa looked at him. The change from lover to employer had been instantaneous. One moment, loving her with a hunger that had seemed as great as hers and the next, impatient; preoccupied with time passing and the delay to that day's shooting schedule.

There had been no opportunity to talk. The cab had arrived just as she had got downstairs and the pilot had been waiting beside the plane when they had got to the landing strip. There had been no damage, he had said in answer to Grant's anxious query. The forced landing hadn't given her a scratch and she had flown like a bird when he had picked her up and flown in from the farm even earlier.

Lissa looked at him now, sitting next to Grant as the plane droned on, totally unaware of the change that had taken place in the relationship between his two passengers, just as she would have been totally unaware if she hadn't been able to feel the renewed stamp of Grant's possession on every centimetre of her skin.

'Can you take some notes?' His actor's voice exactly pitched to compensate for engine noise, Grant spoke to her without turning his head.

'Of course.' She fought down a sudden spurt of resentment as she fumbled for the book and pencil she had earlier picked up from the bedroom floor where they had been since Grant had sent them flying from her hands the previous night.

She was being irrational in expecting him to treat her as anything other than his secretary. That, after all, was what everyone still thought she was—the man piloting the plane included. He would hardly be likely to break the news now. There would probably be some sort of announcement later, after they had had a chance to talk and decide what form it should take. It would be quite a surprise—telling everyone she was his wife. She wondered how Sandy would react and smiled as she visualised the continuity girl's expression when she discovered there was going to be one less 'Hen' in the Coop for the rest of the filming.

She poised her pencil, ready to start work. 'I'm ready.'

'Okay, now get this down,' he said impersonally. 'We scrub the scenes between Riel and Gabriel Dumont scheduled for today. When we get back, pencil them in on the chart as a possibility for Thursday and check that René and Clarke are both available. Call their agents,' he added as an aside as she made a note beside the actors' names. 'Today we start the scenes with Alys. Long shot, close shot and master shot of her arrival and a reverse for the funeral. Use the same camera angles to emphasise the irony of lost hopes.'

The rapid, staccato notes went on and on, forcing her to clear her mind of everything so that her pencil could fly unimpeded across the pages. The words themselves did not make any sense, he was going too fast for her to have time to think about their meaning, all that mattered was that they should be translated into crisp, sharp shorthand outlines, ready to type up the moment they got back.

He finished just as the clearing with the trailers and the lifelike set came into view ahead and beneath them. The sun was rising now, blood red and rapidly coming up above the horizon. First no more than a rim on the horizon, then a flat half circle and then a full globe, drawing perceptibly away from the surface of the earth.

In black and white, reduced by distance and by the sheer physical size of the sky above it, the location could have been a primitive settlement, lost in the forest, and the comparison was heightened even more when a few Eskimo-like figures emerged to look up at them and point as the plane circled like a great bird and came in to land behind its shadow on the frozen lake.

The pilot cut the engine. 'Right, come on.' Grant was out and urging her to follow the moment the prop stopped. 'Okay, Stu, you're gone. See you later.'

'Where's he going?' Tugged by the slipstream as the plane started up and taxied for a take-off, Lissa had to fight to keep her footing on the thin layer of ridged snow covering the ice.

'Back to Saskatoon.' Grant was already striding towards the built-up pressure ridge of ice between them and the shore.

'But why?' She stumbled after him.

'To get Morgan, of course. She flew in to

Saskatoon last night. Rather than have her drive on to Rosglen, I said I'd send a plane to get her. She's waiting there. For God's sake, Lissa!' He stopped as the thought struck him. 'Don't say you didn't get everything down! The Alys scenes,' he stressed. 'Morgan's playing Alys, that's why I've had to change the schedule. Her agent got a message through on Friday. She's been offered a part in Hollywood, so I agreed to change our schedule so that she would be free to accept. For God's sake,' he repeated, 'don't say you didn't get all that?'

'Yes, I got it.' Torn between humiliation and the beginnings of a deep fiery rage, Lissa numbly stood and watched him walk on. How was he to know that, in order to keep up with his dictation, she had not been able to absorb the sense of what he said? She had been thinking about her shorthand and the problems of forming crisp, easily decipherable outlines in a moving plane.

Of course Morgan was playing Alys. She had known that, but it just hadn't connected in her head. Just as it had not connected that the rough schedule of scenes between Alys and her fur-trapper husband would be played by Morgan and Grant himself.

'Lissa!' He had noticed she wasn't following. 'Come on! We've already lost half a day's shooting time!' He headed towards the clearly anxious figure of Norris Potter waiting on the shoreline, easily recognisable in the trendy Beatle cap he always insisted on wearing in spite of the punishing cold.

'Bring those notes across to me in Norris's trailer directly they're typed up.'

He joined the director and they walked off to start the production meeting that would have taken place the previous night if bad weather had not forced them down.

Lissa burned as she got to the Hen Coop and started typing. She couldn't imagine anyone except Morgan for whom Grant would be prepared to alter the entire shooting schedule. Time was money and time was ticking rapidly away.

'Call agents and check that actors free for later dates.' She went on automatically transcribing her shorthand notes. She would have to fly to Rosglen to do that. There was no telephone on location and the radio was kept for emergencies. No wonder Grant had been so anxious to make that extra telephone call from the hotel. No wonder he had made quite sure that she wouldn't overhear. It *must* have been to Morgan in Saskatoon, explaining why he couldn't fly to meet her. It wouldn't have done to have kept Morgan waiting without a word.

'Alys goes to him and draws his head against her breast. Cut to close shot of her face.' Just as she had gone to him and, in the course of the night, drawn his head against her breast, wondering if it would still be the same to feel his lips against it and hardly daring to believe it when it was. Had the expression on her face been the one Grant would want to see on Morgan's when it came to the filming? she wondered miserably.

She went on typing the notes for Alys's funeral,

to be shot out of sequence immediately after the filming of her arrival at the settlement as a young bride. 'Use the same camera angles to emphasise the irony of lost hopes.'

And they were lost. Lost, dead, gone. For a moment she had thought—she had scarcely known what she had thought as she had paced the floor of her hotel room, excruciatingly aware of Grant in the room next door—that perhaps he had flown down to Masseyville because he found the idea of her there alone with Ramsay unbearable. Not that he need have worried. She doubted if she would ever see Ramsay again. Grant's arrival, intentional or otherwise, had taken care of that.

She thumped her anger and humiliation out on the inoffensive portable typewriter.

Work for him for three months and prove that he no longer meant anything to her and then he would give her her divorce. Lissa smiled grimly above the keys. That had been the agreement, and he hadn't broken it. All he had done was fly south to Masseyville to get the secretary he needed to take care of an unexpected change in the production schedule. Exactly the reason he had given her when he arrived. She had been the one who had offered herself to him.

God, what a fool she'd been, and how he must be laughing!

'You're going to go right through the floor if you go on banging away like that!' Sandy had come into the trailer, her round, sandy-coloured curls repeating the roundness of her blue eyes. 'I can see you've been caught up in the general panic!'

'Grant flew down and fetched me,' Lissa said tonelessly.

Sandy began the ritual of taking off her coat and boots and piling them beside Lissa's at the door. 'Like a bear with a sore head, no doubt,' she grinned. 'He's been unapproachable since filming finished Friday—count yourself lucky you weren't here to get your share!—and then when the plane came back from flying you to Rosglen with a message from that Morgan woman saying she wanted the schedule altered, all hell broke loose. People running in all directions, Grant flying back and forth and Norris throwing one of his better temper tantrums. And now you two getting delayed until this morning has made things even worse. The whole crew's hanging around doing nothing, waiting for the lovely Morgan Vale to arrive. It must be costing hundreds!' she ended on a note of satisfaction.

Finishing the new production schedule, Lissa ripped the paper and carbons from the typewriter with a satisfying tearing noise. Sandy glanced across.

'What did happen, by the way? We heard you got forced down. Did you have to spend the night in the plane? Come to think of it, I wouldn't mind doing that myself! Cold, but——' she wriggled her shoulders expressively, 'what a man to have around to keep me warm!'

'Excuse me.' Lissa got up and picked up her coat. 'I've got to take these notes across to Grant.'

'Sit down, will you?' When she got to Norris's trailer, Grant took the typed sheets without turning his head. 'I might want you to take notes. Here you are,' he handed copies of her work to Norris and the lighting cameraman. The young assistant director, sitting subdued in a corner and managing not to look at her, had to reach for his own. 'Now, where were we?' Grant went on. 'Oh, yes. If we're going to get Morgan's scenes in the can so that she can fly out Thursday, we're going to have to do it this way round.'

Everything was for Morgan, Lissa noticed as she took a chair and sat with her eyes fixed on a point somewhere above the back of Grant's head. Nothing must be allowed to interfere with Morgan flying out from the location in time to take the part she had been offered in Hollywood—even if it did cost 'hundreds of dollars.' Perhaps Grant had been expecting to fly in to Saskatoon and meet her himself the previous night, in which case their own forced landing had probably cost him more than a half day's filming.

The meeting went on endlessly, building on Grant's notes and giving Norris and the cameraman the chance to make their contributions. The only people who had nothing to say were herself and the young assistant director, clearly still suffering from the tongue-lashing rumour had it he had received from Grant after the impromptu party in this same trailer the other night.

The meeting went on through lunch—soup, sandwiches and coffee brought across from the

catering hut—and only stopped when the sound of
a plane flying in over the lake indicated that
Morgan had, at long last, arrived. At a nod from
Grant, Lissa joined the tail end of the procession
trailing out across the snow to meet her. She looked
lovely.

'Darling!' She immediately flung her arms
around Grant's neck, all flying blonde hair and
fantastic violet eyes in a silver fox fur coat and hat.
'I couldn't believe it when my agent called and said
you were prepared to go to all this trouble just for
little me!'

Hatless in spite of the biting cold, Grant bent
and kissed her cheek. 'In which case, you won't
mind if we put you straight to work,' he said drily.
'Now Norris you already know, and this is Sam
Phillips, the lighting cameraman. . . .' He went on
introducing them until, last in the line, he came to
Lissa. 'And this is Lissa Benson, my secretary.'

'Lissa?' Not having seen her since Barbados,
Morgan looked at her doubtfully. 'But I thought
. . .?' she started on a rising note.

'You're not here to think,' Grant interjected
roughly. At least he treated other people as cal-
lously as he treated her. It was some consolation,
but not much, as Lissa saw the way Morgan's face
glowed as she looked up at him and heard the purr
of possession as she slipped her gloved hand
through his arm.

'Darling,' she said, 'that beard! It makes you
look positively primitive!'

The second consolation was that not even

Morgan could look her usual glamorous self in the canvas-like brown dress and cloak Wardrobe had supplied for her. Authenticity was to be the hallmark of this production, Grant said firmly when she complained. The outfit had been copied from pictures of the period and was to be worn whether it scratched her skin or not.

He had also changed. His jeans and shirt had given way to the leather fringed jerkin, pants and soft moccasin type boots with leather lacings around the legs worn by the Hudson Bay Company's trappers a hundred years earlier. Together, it was almost impossible to recognise Grant Ferries and the glamorous Morgan Vale in the two people walking through their first scene under Norris's direction.

And she was good, Lissa had to acknowledge that. Once work started, all the exaggerated mannerisms disappeared and she gave it her total concentration. It was no coincidence that of all the starlets with whom Grant's name had been associated during the years, Morgan had been one of the very few to make the transition to first class actress in her own right. Carefully made up to give the impression of no make-up and with her ash-blonde hair scraped back under a linen cap above her pale face, she *was* Alys Massignac, the young wife brought west into the wilds of nineteenth-century Saskatchewan and slowly dying of consumption while her husband blindly worked out his obsession with the Riel rebellion.

'Right, that's a wrap!' After a long afternoon's

work, the last scene ended and, at a nod from
Norris, the young assistant repeated his nightly
litany as the sun dropped beneath the horizon,
leaving a flaring arrowhead of black and crimson
streaked across an opalescent sky.

'Thank God! I'm freezing!' Morgan stood up
and walked away from the graveside setting,
rubbing her arms underneath her cloak. 'Do we
have drinks now, darling?'

She looked up at Grant, huge in his rough
leather costume against the dying light. Lissa saw
him pause and then his face cleared and he smiled.
'I guess so,' he said indulgently. 'We can't have
you really dying of pneumonia! The plane can wait
for once for the rushes and,' he glanced across at
Norris, 'we'll have the production meeting later
tonight, if that's okay with you.'

'No problem, mate!' Norris was quick to agree,
just as quick as he was to take up a position on
Morgan's other side.

Morgan took off the plain linen cap and tossed
her blonde hair free around her face. 'Well,' she
said, 'what are we waiting for?'

Lissa stood and watched them go: Morgan obviously enjoying the attention of two men and be-
stowing her responses equally. No, not quite, she
noticed with a quick stab. Morgan might be talking
and smiling across at Norris, but it was Grant's
arm through which she firmly tucked her hand.

'Aren't you going?' Sandy came up beside Lissa
and nodded in the direction of the trio.

'No!' Wild horses wouldn't have dragged her

into Norris's trailer where the three of them were now disappearing. 'Aren't you?'

'After the rousting Dave and I got after the party the other evening, you must be joking!' Sandy laughed. 'Besides, there are some occasions when we more humble members of the crew are not invited, and this is definitely one of them!' She dropped her voice. 'I wonder which one of them she fancies. Me, I'd take Grant, but then you never know. Norris has got a movie coming up with United and it wouldn't do her any harm to get in on that.'

Lissa bent and picked up her folding stool. 'Perhaps she's not interested in either one of them.'

'Mm,' Sandy snorted, 'I wouldn't bet on it! Anyway,' she changed the subject, 'Dave and I were planning on having supper together.' She nodded in the direction of the young assistant now walking towards them with an eager smile on his face. 'Why don't you join us? At least we've got one thing for which to thank Miss Morgan Vale— we've got some spare time tonight before the production meeting. It's one law for the rich and another for the poor, as you might say. Hi, Dave,' she added as the assistant director reached them, 'Lissa's going to eat with us.'

Lissa wondered if Sandy also saw the quick flicker of disappointment on Dave Hammond's face, gone as soon as it appeared but there just the same. Morgan wasn't the only one having her romantic inclinations thwarted by the presence of a third person. 'You two go on ahead,' she offered, 'I'll eat later.'

'Nonsense!' Dave gallantly put an arm around her shoulders. 'Come with us. You look as if you could use some company!'

Fifteen minutes later, sitting in the prefabricated catering hut with her meal in front of her in a pre-formed plastic tray and Dave and Sandy chattering on about a shared interest in old movies, Lissa pondered on the difference between this evening and all the other evenings before Morgan had arrived on the location. There was indeed one law for the rich and another for the poor, as Sandy claimed. Tonight, everything could wait. The pilot standing by to fly the rushes to Rosglen and the nightly production meeting when all members of the crew were called together to discuss the detailed schedule for the next day's filming—everything could be delayed to suit Morgan.

She contrasted it with Grant's attitude to her. Morgan had only to say she was cold and the unit's entire routine could be changed, whereas she, after one drink at the end of a bitterly cold day's filming, had not only been accused of being incapable of doing her work properly but of starting a flirtation as well.

The door opened and she looked up. Would Grant react now if he saw her there with Dave? But it wasn't Grant, just a group of stagehands and electricians. Not that she need have worried. Grant was hardly likely to appear yet. He was still with Morgan with Norris playing the role of the unwanted third person, just as she was playing it with Dave and Sandy.

She took a mouthful of her steak. The standard of location catering was excellent, with fruit and fresh vegetables flown in to supplement the huge deep-freeze run off the units generators, but tonight everything was tasteless. She tried to eat, tried to do anything to take her mind off the thought of Grant with Morgan, even to the extent of trying to take part in a discussion about the relative merits of the first, silent version of the Garbo movie *Anna Karenina* compared to the later sound one, but it was impossible. A picture of Grant with Morgan's arm threaded through his ran through everything.

The door swung open again. This time it was Dave who looked up with a guilty start, and this time it was Grant with Morgan and a smiling Norris in tow. Morgan had her fur coat thrown on over her costume, but Grant had changed from his filming clothes into his usual working uniform of woollen shirt and tightly fitting jeans. How surprising that he had been able to bear tearing himself away from Morgan's company even long enough to do that, Lissa noted grimly, especially when it must have meant leaving her alone with Norris. But then Grant didn't have to be with a woman to leave his stamp on her. She had proved that herself last night.

After two years, she had gone to him as if no more than hours had passed, practically begging him to make love to her. He had no more believed the flimsy excuse of notebook and pencil than she had. How gratifying it must have been for him to find that he could still exercise his old power over her in spite of everything she had claimed. What a boost for his male ego!

She stood, abruptly, leaving her meal unfinished on her tray. 'Excuse me,' she said to Dave and Sandy, 'I have to get back and get on with my work.'

'Lissa!' She heard him call as she was heading for the door, but she ignored him with a rigid back. Let him draw what conclusion he liked from her abrupt departure—that she was embarrassed at having him find her there with Dave; that his appearance had brought on an attack of guilty conscience. Let him think anything except the one true reason—that it was unbearable to stay and see him there with Morgan.

CHAPTER EIGHT

THREE days, two days, one day—just twenty-four more hours and Morgan would be gone and life would become, if not painless, at least something she could endure. And with a part waiting for her in Hollywood, there was no way Morgan could stay longer even if she wanted to. Her contract with Hollywood was signed, as she had lost no time in announcing loudly to all and sundry. After years of working only in the Canadian film industry, it was her big breakthrough on to the international scene. She had no intention of missing it and, on top of that, the scenes here with Massignac and Alys were well up to, even ahead of, schedule.

There was just one more to do the following morning—an emotional dialogue between the fur-trapper and his wife establishing just how rigorous life must have been for any gently bred woman who came out West to join her man at the end of the nineteenth century.

Like most of the other segments, it would be shot out of sequence, but when the film was finally edited, it would come shortly after Alys's arrival at the settlement when she realised she would be left completely on her own in a strange country with the elements of rebellion building up around her, while Massignac went out by dog-sled to check his trap lines.

Sitting in the heavily insulated Hen Coop—barely warm this evening with an arctic storm blowing up outside—Lissa typed the notes for the last schedule to contain Morgan's name. From tomorrow, life would be bearable and, as far as watching this last scene between Grant and Morgan was concerned, she would concentrate on the dogs. They had been flown in that afternoon; eight magnificent Siberian huskies, handsome, intelligent—and totally untrustworthy, their handler had warned in the general surge to go and pet them. They were outside now, small white mounds in the blowing snow, apparently oblivious to cold.

The door of the trailer opened, but Lissa scarcely bothered to look up. It had to be Sandy. Jane, the make-up girl, was in the middle of a torrid affair with the lighting cameraman—if anything could be called torrid in these temperatures—and, after the first night, Morgan had moved out of the Hen Coop.

'Hi!' Sandy brought a draught of freezing air in with her. 'Gee, it's cold in here! It must be the direction of the wind. I think I'll keep these on.' She shed her boots but kept the thick blue felt liners. She also kept her padded coat and woolly hat. 'Those poor dogs,' she said with feeling. 'I passed them on my way across.'

'I suppose they're used to it.' Lissa went on typing and the sound of Sandy's typewriter joined in from the far end of the trailer. The usual evening routine; the producer's assistant in pants and a thick sweater typing up his notes and the continuity girl in a parka and brilliant orange hat, adding to the vast volume of detail that she scrupulously transcribed each night. All part of the glamour of location filming.

Lissa supposed she should be used to it—just like the huskies. She broke off and tried to rub some of the cold out of her hands. She also supposed she should be used to the pairing off that always seemed to take place on location. That, after all, had been the cause of some of her most violent arguments with Grant; her refusal to take his word that stories romantically linking him with his current leading lady were totally untrue. A kiss wasn't an affair, he had said contemptuously, when she had thrust newspaper pictures in front of him.

But although Grant had denied the evidence of the publicity pictures, it did seem as if being brought together in an out-of-the-way location, with none of the restraints of home, heightened the emotional responses.

After a brief flirtation with the leading man, Jane, the make-up girl, had disappeared into the arms of the lighting cameraman, and Sandy was also being openly pursued.

'Isn't she fabulous?' Dave had come up to Lissa during one of the interminable waiting periods in the filming, talking to her but his eyes firmly fixed on Sandy standing beside Grant. 'Don't you think she looks just like a young Ingrid Bergman?'

No, she was a dear, but never, by the wildest stretch of the imagination, could Lissa see an Ingrid Bergman of any age when she looked at Sandy's round, rather pug-nosed face. Her hair might be roughly the same colour, but there all resemblance stopped. But then, they said, love was blind; blind and almost always doomed, just as hers had been and just, she suspected, as Dave's would be. For all their shared interest in old movies, Sandy never showed the slightest sign of regarding him as a young Humphrey Bogart. Indeed, Lissa had the feeling that there was already a boy-friend back in Toronto.

'Dave!' At that moment, Grant had caught sight of them and called Dave across. Why did he seem to mind so much who she was talking to? Surely he had proved everything he needed to prove about his hold on her that night at the hotel and, on top of that, he now had Morgan.

Morgan had come into the Hen Coop on her first night on the location and looked around her with obvious distaste. 'My God,' she drawled, 'is this where we have to sleep?'

'It's not that bad,' Sandy replied pragmatically. 'I've lived in worse. Your bed's over there.' She nodded in the direction of two bunks kept for visiting actresses and partially screened off from the main cabin. 'After all, you're only here for three nights, aren't you?'

Morgan's face became grim and determined. 'We'll see about that,' she said. She was there that night, but after that she disappeared, coming in early in the morning and using her bunk space as a wardrobe but never sleeping there.

Listening in on a conversation between two of the electricians, Lissa gathered bets were being taken on whether Grant or Norris was the lucky recipient of her favours, but Lissa knew. Both Grant and Norris had their own trailers and, whichever one she favoured, Morgan was using discretion, but Lissa had no doubts and Morgan had confirmed it.

'You *are* the girl from Barbados, aren't you?' she asked one morning.

'Yes, that's right.'

They were alone in the trailer; Morgan critically surveying herself in the mirror and waiting for Jane to come back from breakfast and make her up, and Lissa, later than she usually was, struggling with her boots.

'I thought so.' Morgan was satisfied. 'I've wondered from time to time exactly what happened to you.' It was not a charitable concern, that was obvious.

'Well, now you know.' Face flushed, Lissa went on battling with laces that refused to go through eyelet holes, breathless and uncomfortable from the effort of stooping over in her thick padded coat.

'Yes, now I know,' Morgan said complacently. She leaned forward and tweezed a stray eyebrow into line. 'Did you know there was a rumour about at one time that you two were married?' She went on tweezing, apparently intent on her appearance but her eyes never leaving Lissa. Why didn't somebody come in and stop this conversation? 'Nothing definite, although I wouldn't have been surprised. Grant was certainly showing all the signs of making a complete fool of himself on that bloody island. All those romantic early morning swims going on before I left. It was pathetic, really, but I can remember being quite upset! But then,' her face changed; spiteful and vindictive one moment, satisfied the next, '—then I heard that you'd rather dropped out of sight.'

Yes, that was true. The publicity departments of the various film companies had made sure of that. It would most certainly not have done for a rising sex symbol to be saddled with a wife. Pursuing her career on this side of the Atlantic, Morgan would not have been one of the few people to have known about their marriage. And she would most certainly not have known that it had been a glimpse of her in Grant's arms that had brought their marriage to an end.

Morgan slowly stood up, smoothing the rough skirt of her dress with long white hands. The princess and the swineherd's daughter, Lissa thought, looking at their reflections in the mirror. Morgan composed and beautiful in spite of her homespun dress and she totally shapeless in her padded coat with a red face and redder hair hanging in untidy strands after the effort of tying her boots.

Morgan studied her. 'You're still stuck on him, aren't you?'

'I don't know what you're talking about.' Lissa started to turn away, but the attack in Morgan's voice made her stop.

'Don't give me that!' she said contemptuously. 'It's as plain as the nose on your face that you're still carrying a torch for him. But you're too late!' The white hands moved up from the skirt to the closely fitting bodice of the dress, almost caressing as they then smoothed from breast to waist beneath a face now filled with memories of past pleasures. 'You should have got him when you could, you know. It was quite sharp of you to get this job with him, but you're too late. With a man like Grant, you don't get a second chance.'

Someone had come in at that moment. Either Sandy or the make-up girl, Lissa could not recall. What she could recall—could still see in absolute, infinite clarity even now as she sat in the trailer, typing up the notes for Alys's last appearance in the filming, was the face of the woman who was to

play her filled with the sensuous satisfaction of
successful lovemaking and talking about Grant.
There was absolutely no doubt in whose trailer
Morgan had spent all but the first night since she
had been on location.

Lissa went on typing. Two more pages and she
would be finished with Grant's notes for the scene
where Massignac went off to his trap lines leaving
Alys alone, and then she would never have to type
either the name Alys or Morgan Vale again.

The door of the trailer opened again, but she
took no notice. This time, it was probably Jane.
The romance with the cameraman seemed to be
cooling and the make-up girl was spending a little
more time in the Hen Coop than she had been
doing. Lissa typed harder, anxious to get the work
done for the regular production meeting later that
evening.

'I want to talk to you!' It wasn't the inrush of
cold air that made the hair on the nape of her neck
prickle, it was the voice, harsh and compelling, that
brought every nerve alert.

'I'll be finished in a minute.' She went on typing,
refusing to look up but feeling his presence behind
her shoulder as acutely as if they had been touching.

'I haven't come here for the notes.' There was a
pause, then, 'Sandy!' he cut in above the clacking
of the typewriters, 'perhaps you'd give us a few
minutes?'

Sandy's machine abruptly stopped. 'What? Oh,
yes . . . sure. No problem.'

Out of the corner of her eye Lissa saw Sandy,

practically open-mouthed, scrabble her notes and papers together and head for the door. There was another pause while she struggled with her boots and then the door slammed shut.

'Now stop that damned racket!' A hand came across her shoulder down on to the keys, trapping hers beneath it and sending a shock along her arms.

Now she swung to face him, pulling her hands away and looking up at him with hard, bright eyes. 'Why?' she taunted. 'Have you decided to stop being a slavedriver? I thought the only thing you were interested in was work!' She refused to allow herself to be affected by the sight of him, towering above her with his jacket open and his throat bare against the freezing weather. The tiny hairs on his chest gleamed in the open neck of his shirt. He smelled cold and looked hard, just like the world outside.

'I do occasionally think of things other than work.' He smiled, crinkling the fan of tiny lines around his eyes.

'I'm sure!' Damn him for that smile. It took all her willpower not to weaken even though reason told her it was caused by memories of Morgan.

'And what exactly does that mean?' The smile vanished, leaving him hard and watchful.

'Ask the crew.' Although whether any member of the crew would be willing to tell him about the bets being taken on whether Morgan was spending her nights in his trailer or in Norris's was a different matter.

'I don't *ask* the crew anything,' he snapped, 'I tell them! What I want to ask *you* is why you're avoiding me!'

'I would hardly say being at your elbow all day is avoiding you,' she answered. 'And that doesn't count the time at the production meetings in the evenings. Now, if you'll excuse me. . . .' She went to turn back to the typewriter, but he stopped her, his grip paralysing on her shoulder.

'I told you to stop that!' he warned. 'Now tell me!'

'Why? What do you want me to say?' she blazed. 'That you've won? Because if that's what you think, I can assure you that you're wrong!

'Won?' For an instant he seemed genuinely puzzled.

'The other night. . . .' Lissa refused to be more explicit. 'I suppose you think that meant something.' It was surprising how good an actress she could be; almost as good as Morgan. 'Well, let me tell you something. It didn't mean a thing. You mean nothing in my life—nothing, do you hear! If it hadn't been for the forced landing . . . for everything . . .' she sketched a gesture, 'do you think I would have let you come near me?' Choked by tears she refused to let him see, she wrenched her shoulder from his hand and started typing, not knowing and not caring which keys she hit, just grateful for the chance to hide her face.

'In that case, there's no more to be said, is there?' Although low, Grant's voice carried easily above the chatter of the machine. 'I'll expect those notes in my trailer in ten minutes.'

She heard him leave the trailer and abandoned all pretence of typing. He could go, but there was no way she could leave so easily. They were miles from Rosglen and from the larger centre of Saskatoon and her car was even farther away in Masseyville. In insisting she fly all the way back to the location, Grant had trapped her as effectively as if it had been planned. She wiped her eyes and blew her nose; then she pulled the ruined paper from the typewriter and put in more. If she got on with her work she could ignore the awful truth that the main reason she was staying on at the location was because of Grant.

She had to steel herself to take the notes across to his trailer and then sit down in her usual place as his secretary and wait for the rest of the unit to assemble for the nightly production meeting. She had to give him credit for discretion. In spite of all the time she spent there, there was no sign of Morgan in the trailer. No overlooked bottle of perfume, nothing hanging in the wardrobe space, just Morgan herself, sitting in on the meeting by right as a leading performer in the next day's shooting and then not even beside Grant but next to Norris.

Her own relationship with the director had not improved since the day they had met and he had mistaken her for yet another fan throwing herself at Grant's head, and she wondered how Morgan could bear to have him sit so close to her. To her, he was creepy; overweight and pudgy with a leer rather than a smile and hot bedroom eyes. She doubted if she had exchanged ten words with him since she had arrived on the location. Morgan, on the other hand, seemed totally unperturbed that his thigh was resting against hers, and Lissa wondered what Grant's reaction was to that.

She glanced at him, but the beard made it impossible to read his face as he abruptly called everyone to order and the last production meeting concerning Morgan got under way.

It was still Morgan, however, who was kept back on the pretext of dialogue rehearsals for the next day's shooting when the rest of them trooped out into the freezing night. Morgan and, of course, Norris to direct them; how Grant must have resented that!

She was out on location deliberately early the following morning, determined to avoid all chance of another spiteful *tête-à-tête* with Morgan and glad to be out of the chilly but stuffy trailer into the cold bright day. For the first time in days, Jane had spent the whole night in the Hen Coop and the atmosphere had been decidedly tense.

Outside, a fierce north wind had blown the storm south during the night, leaving the snow frozen in fantastic, high-crested waves with delicate, wafer-thin ice edges. It was still, so still that the crack of a tree in the nearby forest sounded like a rifle shot and the voices of the crew out on the frozen lake carried easily. They were working beyond the pressure ridge of ice, clearing the snow away so that the plane could make the flight to Rosglen later in

the day. Others were in front of the cottage used
for the scenes between Alys and Massignac and so
realistic that it took a long, close look to realise
that everything, from the sod roof to the mud
chinking between the heavy hand-hewn logs, was,
in fact, made of synthetic, man-made materials.

The cameraman was already there, setting up his
angles and checking them with Norris, and so,
Lissa saw immediately, was Grant, towering above
the rest, rough-hewn and powerful in his leather
costume. She fished her shades out of her pocket
and put them on, grateful for the excuse of brilliant
sunlight reflecting from the snow. With her eyes
hidden behind the glasses, no one could tell what
an effort it was to go and take her usual place at
his side. Grant didn't speak.

'You forgot this.' One of the grips came up with
her stool and she thanked him. Grant took no
notice.

The dog team arrived, harnessed to the loaded
sled in which Massignac was to be seen leaving for
his trap lines. Shaggy creatures, almost up to
Lissa's waist, it was hard to believe the dogs could
be vicious as they leaned into the traces, bright-
eyed with their tongues lolling out in engaging
smiles, eager to do the job they had been bred for.
When their shots had been done, they would be
the first ones out of the location on the plane,
which would then come back for Morgan.

'Keep away from them!' Their handler, wearing
a false beard and dressed in the clothes for which
he was to double for Grant in all the driving shots,

shouted a general warning. 'Don't go near them and don't pet them.'

Sensing the delay, the dogs dropped into the snow and lay there while the work of setting up the first shot went on. Lissa smiled. Filming, as she had discovered, was a process of interminable waiting punctuated by short, sharp bursts of frenzied energy. It was hard to maintain interest during those long waiting periods and harder still to spring into a state of peak efficiency and concentration when the camera actually started rolling. The dogs were sensible to save their energies.

Morgan arrived with Jane—ostentatiously circling round the cameraman. Then, with an expressive lift of eyebrows in their direction, Sandy scuttled past to take her place beside Norris. Lissa saw Dave's face brighten.

Morgan wore her fur coat over her costume. As usual, she looked lovely but, for once, she was less than the centre of attention. Grant and Norris—the only two to whom she chose to speak—acknowledged her arrival with only perfunctory good mornings. Everyone was preoccupied with setting up the shots for the sequence with the dog-sled. Grant was to be filmed going up to it, then there would be a cut away from the close shot and it would be the handler who was seen actually driving it away.

'And it's likely to be a one-shot deal,' Lissa heard him saying on the other side of Grant. 'Those dogs might look like pussycats, but once they get going, they take a heap of stopping and they won't do the same thing over and over!'

'In that case, we'd better set up a couple more camera positions, mate,' Norris said practically. 'A hand held there and the Arriflex on a tripod shooting from the trees. That way, we should get enough footage in one take whatever happens.'

The three men walked off towards the trees fringing the location, collecting the sound man and the cameraman on the way. Lissa toyed with the idea of going with them but stayed on her stool. If Grant had wanted her, he would have said, and the less she had to do with Grant, especially with Morgan present, the better for her peace of mind.

She found herself watching Morgan. Although professional enough to understand the lack of attention she was getting, as a woman she obviously resented it. Morgan Vale was not used to taking second place. Her face wore a sulky look as she wandered from one group to another and Lissa wondered why she had come out so early when she knew the dog sequence was to be filmed first. To wring the most she could out of her last few hours with Grant, no doubt. Tonight she would be flown out of the location and tomorrow she would be on her way to Hollywood. Lissa refused to think farther ahead than that.

The next time she saw Morgan, it would be in a picture in a newspaper or a magazine, perhaps with Grant, perhaps not, but certainly above a story announcing that she was to be his wife. The three-month testing period Grant had imposed for their divorce had been a farce—a cruel joke. His way of making use of the fantastic coincidence of the unit choosing Masseyville for its first location shots to revenge himself on her for walking out on him. He had already made up his mind about a divorce. Seeing him with Morgan, waiting hour after hour each night for Morgan to come back to the Hen Coop and imagining her with Grant, how could she any longer possibly have any doubts? She had been mad to think, even when Grant had been holding her in his arms with his body making hers complete, that he had any feeling left for her. As Morgan had so rightly pointed out, with a man like Grant, there was no second chance.

So she, perhaps, was the only one to notice when Morgan started to walk towards the dogs. Left alone on the outside of the group, they had been lying quietly enough, but with Morgan making her way towards them, they were stirring suspiciously and, as Lissa watched, the lead dog got stiffly to its feet. Standing in the brilliant light, with every hair in its huge ruff displayed around its neck, it was clearly dangerous, but Morgan either failed to notice or else chose not to see.

'Beauty tames the beast!' Lissa could practically see the caption ballooning above her head.

Had Morgan been there when the handler had issued his general warning against touching them? No, she had not. Lissa remembered seeing her arrive with Jane after the dogs had sunk down in the snow. She started to rise, scarcely feeling the stool fall against the back of her legs. 'Morgan!' she called. 'Morgan! Stop! Don't go any farther!'

Perhaps above all others, her voice was the one guaranteed to have the least effect. Morgan went on. 'Morgan, don't!' Dimly aware of other people turning in their direction and of the handler, with Grant and Norris, emerging from the trees, Lissa began to run, hampered by her heavy boots but yards ahead of anyone else. 'Morgan, don't!' Straining against his trace, the lead dog's teeth snapped inches away from them and all sound was lost in a cacophony of barking as Lissa caught hold of Morgan's shoulder and pulled her back. She fell in a flying tangle of fox fur coat and silver hair.

'How dare you!' Her face contorted in a spasm of sheer rage, Morgan looked up at her. 'How dare you do that to me?'

'What the hell's going on?' Outstripping the rest, Grant raced up to them. 'Are you all right?' He barely glanced at Lissa's white face.

'I'm fine!' She need not have bothered to reply. Grant was already bending and gently helping Morgan to her feet.

Practically hysterical, she buried her face against his chest. 'Darling,' she sobbed, 'did you see what happened? She deliberately pushed me!'

Above her head, Grant looked grim. 'Yes, I saw.' He called to Norris hurrying up to them. 'Get the shots with the dogs done first and get them out of here. I'm taking Morgan back to my trailer for a while.'

Holding her like a child who has been unjustly treated, he half led, half carried the sobbing Morgan off. Lissa stood and watched. How could he be so blind? He had looked at her as if she was a criminal, and yet if it hadn't been for her, he wouldn't be taking Morgan to his trailer, he would be flying her to hospital. The dogs were still snarling and snapping among themselves; it hardly took too much imagination to know what would have happened if Morgan had gone on just one or two more steps and they had pulled her down. But then who had ever said love wasn't blind when it came to blame?

'Okay, people—show's over! Let's get down to work. We'll start with the shot of the dogs going towards the forest. Matt, you'll double for Grant.' Norris cut into the hiatus with a string of orders and the group began to break up and move away.

'Lissa, are you okay?' Going against the stream, Sandy came up to her.

'Yes, I'm fine.' Lissa watched Grant open the door of his trailer and show Morgan inside. 'Apart from having made a complete idiot of myself!'

'Rubbish!' Sandy said practically. 'Everyone saw what happened. Lucky for her you were close enough to stop her—silly fool!'

'Grant doesn't seem to see it like that.'

'Sure he does. Oh . . .' Sandy grinned and clicked her teeth, 'don't take any notice of all that.' She jerked her head in the direction of the trailer. 'I sometimes forget how new you are to this. Morgan's important, right? She's not the star, but as far as this morning's filming is concerned, she's vital, and we'll be ready for her in about half an hour when we've finished with the dogs. So if she's in a state where she either can't—or won't—work, it's going to cost us time and time means money. It all boils down to dollars and cents!'

'Continuity!' Norris interrupted with an angry shout. 'When you've quite finished socialising! We haven't got all day!'

Sandy grinned. 'See what I mean?' She opened her folder of continuity notes and started to walk away. 'Grant's got to take her side. She won't dare be anything except co-operative by the time he's finished telling her how wonderful she is! Look, I've got to run. See you later.'

There was logic in what she said, Lissa considered grimly, but what Sandy didn't know was that Grant really did think Morgan was wonderful and was probably only too pleased to have the excuse of a few more minutes alone with her. For them, time was short. Morgan would be on the first stage of her journey to Hollywood that evening and their next meeting could be weeks, or even months, away. What was going on in the trailer now was probably more like a scene from the old film, *Brief Encounter*, than a producer pacifying his leading lady.

The filming of the dog sequence started with the handler standing in for Grant on the first long shots. Irrelevant to what was going on and at a loss without Grant's constant stream of comments and asides to note down in her book, Lissa stood numbly watching. But even the dogs couldn't hold her attention and she found her mind constantly wandering to the trailer and what might be going on inside.

Was Grant being as patient and understanding with Morgan as he had once been with her? she wondered miserably. In the early days of their marriage, when it had seemed impossible that she would ever get being a housewife organised to her mother's fine art, little things had driven *her* to that same screaming pitch of anger and frustration. Standing there in the snow, she remembered when a far too ambitious recipe had more than proved her limitations as a cook and the first birthday dinner she had ever tried to cook for Grant had ended up being thrown across the room. But instead of being angry, or even amused, Grant had understood, and the birthday dinner had turned into a take-out meal from the nearest Chinese restaurant followed by long slow hours of love in a bed with sagging springs.

There was no bed with sagging springs in the modern, winterised trailer just across from where she stood; just Morgan being consoled with the love she herself had once had.

How ironic it all was! For two years, Lissa had convinced herself that all she wanted was her freedom, but now that it was almost within her grasp, she knew she had never wanted anything less.

She knew instinctively the moment the door of the trailer opened and it was impossible not to look across. Morgan was laughing now and Grant was smiling down at her as they came down the steps: the picture of a man in love.

'I'll want you to come down with me to the

rushes this evening.' Lissa knew she must have been mistaken; he could not possibly have said that as he walked past. Morgan—now turning all her charm on Norris—was flying down with him and she had no intention of witnessing that particular farewell. It was hard enough to get through the day, forcing herself to watch the scenes between Morgan-Alys and Grant-Massignac, but even a day like that had to come to an end and she was certainly not going to prolong the agony.

'Right-ho, love! We'll just get this last one in the can, shall we? A nice close-shot of you watching the old man leave. Do you think you can manage that?' Norris's aggressively Cockney accent drifted across just as the plane came back from taking the dog team and the handler to Rosglen. He was setting up the last shot: a full frame picture of Alys looking out past camera at Massignac going away.

Presumably as a smokescreen, Morgan had been flirting heavily with him all afternoon and now she pouted, fetchingly. 'For you, anything!'

'Two birds in the hand are obviously better than one in the bush!' Sandy had come up beside Lissa and whispered cynically.

'It's one in the hand and two in the bush,' Lissa pointed out. 'And anyway, what do you mean?'

'It's obvious!' Sandy said patiently.

'Well, not to me!'

'Oh, child, child! Where did you get your education in the ways of the real world? Growing up in lotus land stunted your growth!' The maternal tone was completely at odds with the round unlined face under the brilliant orange hat. 'Having done this job with Grant, our lovely leading lady is making sure Norris won't forget her when he starts his contract with Universal in the spring. She might have got one chance in Hollywood, but a second wouldn't do her any harm. It's known as buttering your beetroots,' she finished on a second fractured metaphor.

But Lissa wasn't interested in metaphors, fractured or not. 'I didn't know Norris was going to Hollywood.'

'You must have done.' Sandy frowned. 'But maybe not. Come to think of it, I think that was confirmed on Friday as well.' She grinned. 'It's amazing what went on here after you left. Anyway,' she grew businesslike, 'Norris has got this whacking contract with Universal; one film for sure and an option to direct two more. Maybe I should chat him up! I'll be out of work, too, when this is finished. Ugh!' she looked at him and shuddered. 'On second thoughts, p'raps not.'

So Morgan intended to go on working when she was married. Lissa saw the thunderclouds on Grant's face as he went up to her and Norris. 'Can we get started?' she heard him enquire acidly. 'The light's beginning to go.'

In the pause that followed as Jane stepped up with a powder brush and Sandy checked the set of Morgan's shawl for continuity, Lissa studied him. His scenes as Massignac were finished and some time during the course of the afternoon, he had found the time to shave his beard and change.

Standing slightly apart from the rest, clear-cut against the sky, he reminded her so vividly of the man a teenage girl had seen for the first time on a beach that it was almost impossible not to walk towards him.

'Right-ho, then, are we ready?' Norris stopped her involuntary movement. 'Okay then, roll 'em!'

'Speed!'

'Action!'

The scene began. Thirty seconds of total silence as Morgan changed from a spoiled, petulant young woman into a woman, also young, agonising over her separation from the man she loved. Tears came, falling naturally and easily down her cheeks, and Lissa caught her breath. In an hour's time, maybe less, that scene would be played for real when Morgan and Grant parted at Rosglen.

'Cut!'

'Right—that's a wrap!' The lessening of tension as the day's work ended was almost tangible. Morgan had no need to flirt with Norris to get work. She wasn't just a good actress, she was brilliant. Like all the rest, Lissa had been affected by the projection of so much emotion. She shivered as she came back to earth.

'Are you going to stand there all day or are you going to get my notes typed up?' Apparently the one person unaffected by Morgan's skill, Grant came up to her.

She flushed. 'I'll have them ready when you get back.'

'I want them now,' he informed her coldly.

'Ready and on the plane in twenty minutes.'

'I'll bring them across to your trailer.'

'You can give them to me on the plane.'

She couldn't—wouldn't—understand. 'You don't mean you want me to fly down with you?'

'Of course.' He wasn't even looking at her but across her shoulder; probably at Morgan. Lissa could hear her talking in the background and then Norris laughed. 'I've got two days' rushes waiting to be viewed and I may need you.'

'What about Sandy?' Lissa asked desperately. 'Why can't she go?'

The eyes flicked back, icy and deep blue. 'Sandy's got her job and you've got yours,' he snapped. 'Twenty minutes, Lissa.'

CHAPTER NINE

'At least you haven't got to go all the way to Masseyville. You can be thankful for that at least.'

'What?' Concerned with typing up Grant's notes, Lissa scarcely listened. A whole day's work in twenty minutes; it was ridiculous. No, it wasn't. It was Grant. Typically Grant! Determined to be nothing less than letter-perfect, she went typing furiously on.

'Masseyville, you know. Wasn't that where you joined us?' Sandy's voice came across the trailer and Lissa slowed down. 'I thought we were never

going to get there when we went for that first
week's filming. On and on in that awful bus heading into nowhere! I should have known what it
was going to be like out here then, of course.' She
shuddered over her pile of continuity sheets, a city
girl out of her element.

'You were talking about Masseyville?' Lissa
reminded her.

'Was I? Oh, yeah.' Sandy forgot about her vision
of the wilderness. 'It was odd. None of us could
understand why Grant insisted on going there. I
mean, one prairie town looks much the same as
another, doesn't it? Railway tracks, grain elevators
and half a dozen stores: but he would have it, even
though we could have stopped at about ninety-four
other identical places on the way and Masseyville
just meant an extra half day's journey on the bus.'

Lissa stopped typing and began to check her
notes. She knew her fingers wouldn't work, but
even so, she could hardly see the words. The rest
of the crew might have been completely baffled,
but she knew exactly why Grant had chosen
Masseyville. She had been there! Somehow he had
found out where she was and, for some purpose of
his own, he had come after her. Everything she
had thought had been sheer coincidence had been
planned: their first, accidental, meeting had been
no more accidental than a bullseye for an expert
marksman who had lined up on his target.

All the little things that had puzzled her began
to fall into place. How he had known that she could
type, for one, when the last time he had seen her

her typing had been very much of the hack and peck variety. Somehow, he had been checking up on her. In the past two years, while she had been thinking he had no idea where she was, he had been keeping her on a very long, loose rein, and now, for some reason of his own, he had decided to pull that rein in.

And the reason wasn't hard to find. Time cost money in the movie production world and yet Grant had been prepared to drag an entire crew half way across the prairies just to arrange their 'accidental' meeting. It had to be because of Morgan. Since the first flurry of lawyers' letters soon after she had left, there had been no contact, no more talk about a divorce, but now, with Morgan once more very much on the scene, Grant must have decided that the time had come to bring matters to a head. At least he was treating them both equally, Lissa thought grimly as she once more began to type. Finding her on location must have been just as traumatic for Morgan as it had been for her.

She could almost feel it in her heart to feel sorry for her successor. Had Morgan known, she wondered, that when she arrived on location she would find the woman that rumour—and the evidence of her own eyes when she had been watching them on the beach in Barbados—had once wanted to be his wife? Did Morgan perhaps even know that that rumour had once been an established fact? Was still a fact, Lissa reminded herself furiously. The other night, when the renewed stamp of his possession had left her feeling as if she had never left his arms, was more than proof of that.

And for him, she was nothing. An interlude to fill the time until Morgan arrived. One of the stream of women constantly throwing themselves at his head. A joke. A victory. He had only to come back into her life to have her begging him to make love to her. His mouth, his hands, his body had branded her, but inside, his mind had laughed.

At first, the knocking on the trailer door was no more than a reflection of the furious thoughts pounding through her head, but then, above the persistent noise of the typewriter, she heard Sandy go and open it. There was a murmured conversation. Whoever it was—Dave, probably—did not come in.

Sandy shut the door. 'Grant wants to know if you're ready.'

'Yes—just!' Tight-lipped, Lissa ripped the paper and carbons out of the machine, separated them and pushed them into an envelope. Then she went across and put on her boots and coat. She caught Sandy watching her curiously.

'Are you okay?'

She pulled up her hood. She was anything but okay. She was angry, humiliated and depressed. 'Yes, I'm fine,' she said.

The cold had clamped down, a different creature from anything she had ever known before, freezing the hairs on the inside of her nose and numbing her mind to the exclusion of all thought. There was no wind and her breath hung in the air in a white cloud, settling as ice on the fur trim of her hood as she walked through it. In the totally black and white setting of the lake, the plane with its lights and impression of twentieth-century technology looked as out of place as an invader from another galaxy, and Lissa felt equally remote and detached as she walked up the steps.

'There you go!' A bundled up figure pulled the steps away and shut the door behind her.

'Thanks.' It was difficult to speak. Like her mind, which the cold had frozen, her face and lips were numb.

She took a seat at the back and fastened her belt as the engines started up. Most of the other seats were filled, she noticed, as warmth began to percolate and her mind began to work; not just Morgan and Grant as she had expected but Norris and the cameraman as well. With the two actors whose schedule Morgan had interrupted flying back with them, the plane would be full on the return flight. Poor Morgan! With all those people, she wasn't likely to have even the luxury of a few moments alone to say her goodbyes to Grant.

But Morgan was laughing and joking as the plane took off and started on the short flight to Rosglen. She had probably made her adieux in the privacy of Grant's trailer before she left. Just as she herself should leave—tonight, without goodbyes—and go back and try and pick up the threads of her old independent life.

The limousine that had been ordered to take Morgan to Saskatoon on the first stage of her journey south to Hollywood was waiting at the airstrip when they touched down. Poor Morgan, indeed! No one had any need to feel sorry for Morgan, Lissa thought grimly, watching the all-round bestowal of hugs and kisses as she said goodbye. Even the cameraman and the pilot got their share; for Lissa there was just a tight, bright smile and a last shrewd look.

'Right then, let's get to the rushes!' Grant was already walking off in the direction of a second car before Morgan's limousine had barely started up. But why should he need to linger on a last farewell? In less than two months' time, this filming would be finished. He could then join Morgan and their future could begin.

The rushes were, as usual, breathtakingly beautiful in the muted tonal range of colour that had been developed to give a hint of the Canadian wilderness as it must have been a hundred years earlier. All blacks and browns against the dead white of the snow with just the occasional flash of colour, like the violet of Morgan's eyes, huge and appealing as they looked out from the screen. Even the makeshift viewing arrangements in the old movie house could not detract from the impact of those eyes as their expression changed from bewilderment to doubt and then to joy as Alys caught her first sight of the man she loved waiting for her at the end of her long journey to this new life as his wife.

'Great, isn't she, mate?' Lissa heard Norris's whispered comment.

'Fantastic!' She wondered if she had imagined the note of dryness in Grant's voice. But apparently she hadn't. 'That close-up's too overpowering there, though,' he went on. 'Lissa, put a question mark beside it.' He flung the order at her across his shoulder through Norris's surprised protest. 'Shot four-two-seven, take two,' he supplied from memory.

The flight back to the location was taut, with Norris brooding over what he considered to be the injustice of Grant demanding his producer's right to edit and Grant tight-lipped and arrogantly silent. Lissa knew that silence well. It had been the ending of so many of their arguments when, after a bitter interchange of words designed to hurt, he had both failed to convince her that the latest publicity story linking him with yet another leading lady was a complete distortion of the truth, or that she still meant anything in his life.

That had been when he had gone into one of those long, stony silences; avoiding her with his eyes and making it impossible for her to take the first step towards him and those were the arguments that had always been left unresolved until, she supposed, she had walked into their London flat one grey, rainy afternoon and found him with Morgan in his arms.

That had been when she had left—just as she would now have to leave again, she thought, as the plane droned on and the voices of the two actors returning to location were the only thing to break the otherwise total silence.

How ironic it all was! Just at the moment when she thought that time had given her the maturity to cope with a marriage in which there would always be the stress and strain of limelight and endless publicity, Morgan had reappeared and her whole dream had tumbled like a house of cards.

One of the actors laughed—another plus for Morgan. At least two people in the plane were reasonably content. Rescheduling the filming to suit her had given them a four-day holiday with pay and then another four days added on to their original contracts. Where Morgan was concerned, time obviously wasn't money. Just as money had been equally irrelevant when Grant had deliberately brought an entire crew to Masseyville. Had he proved what he had wanted to prove in seeking her out? Had Morgan been impressed?

'Okay, folks, it's seat-belt fastening time! We're coming in to land!' The pilot's voice cut through her speculations as the plane banked and started its descent.

They landed and a blast of cold air hit them as the door was opened from outside. 'Home, sweet home!' The actor playing Louis Riel gave a Gallic shrug. 'It hasn't changed, I see.'

No, it hadn't changed. Lissa got her things together and followed him to the door. But tomorrow there would be at least one change. She would leave. Staying on for the full three months of Grant's mockery of a contract would mean going to Toronto for the post-production work. Staying on *could* mean still being there when Grant's engagement to Morgan was announced. Elizabeth Taylor and Richard Burton, after all, had made no secret of their intentions when they had met on *Cleopatra* even though they had each been married to someone else; why should Morgan Vale and Grant Ferries be any different?

Tired to the bone, her mouth filled with the sour taste of defeat, she walked through the gap that had been bulldozed in the pressure ridge of ice, trying not to see the dull glint of the hair in front of her as Grant walked along with Norris.

'Are you coming for a coffee?' One of the two actors had waited for her to catch up.

'No, I don't think so.' She had had nothing to eat or drink since lunchtime—but suddenly the sheer effort of being sociable was too much for her. The Hen Coop was just ahead, on its own on the edge of the trees. All she wanted was to get there and then curl up in a ball on her bunk with the blankets over her head.

'Okay, then. Goodnight.'

'Goodnight.' She set off across the trampled snow. Ten yards, five yards and she would be there.

'Lissa!' She went on walking. 'Lissa!' Grant's voice followed her across. Oh, God, not now! Not when, in spite of everything, her defence against him was so low that the urge to cry was almost irresistible.

But the last thing she would do was let him see. Schooling her face into a mask of sheer indifference, she turned. 'Yes?' she said. 'What do you want?'

'To talk.' He studied her. 'Is that so remark-
able?'

She fought down a sudden treacherous stirring.
'What about?' she snapped. 'Morgan? You want
to know why I deliberately pushed her in front of
a pack of half wild dogs, I suppose!'

'Don't be ridiculous!' He took a step towards
her, but she backed away.

'So it's not work, then. What is it, Grant?' She
nodded in the direction of the Hen Coop. 'If it's
anything more personal, I hardly think Sandy will
appreciate being turned out again at this time of
night.'

'Then let's not bother her.' He took her arm and
her stomach jack-knifed when she realised he was
leading her in the direction of his own trailer. She
thought of fighting him, but what was the point? It
was over, finished. Whatever Grant might want to
say to her, all she had to say was that she was
leaving—tomorrow, tonight—whenever he would
free the plane to fly her to Rosglen.

She glanced up at him as they walked wordlessly
across the snow. In a shaft of light coming from
the dining hut, his weariness looked as great as
hers. The entire burden of keeping the unit up to
schedule showing in the etching of deep lines on
his face. But Lissa refused to let herself feel sym-
pathy. It had been altering the schedule to suit his
mistress that had put them back. If he had not
been so willing to change the shooting sequence to
suit Morgan, they would be four days ahead of the
point they had now reached. Besides, there was

nothing careworn about the way his fingers gripped her arm, numbing even through the padded layers of her coat, as he propelled her up the steps of his trailer and opened the door.

Neither was there anything of Morgan, she saw as he switched on the light. She must give him credit for that, at least. Surely there should have been a photograph.

'Take off your coat.'

'Why?' She faced him with a spurt of her old spirit. 'I shan't be staying long.'

'Will you please stop playing games?' His voice said his temper was on the edge of breaking point. 'You'll stay as long as it takes us to finish what we have to say to each other. Now give me your coat!' The spirit of resistance spluttered and died. Once more, what was the point? Lissa took off her coat and gave it to him. Grant turned to hang it up. 'Now sit down,' he said.

She chose the farthest chair. The trailer was large with several chairs and a hinged desk folding down from the wall at one end. Please let him sit at the desk, she prayed, and then she would be safe. She crossed her fingers superstitiously. If he sat down at the desk, he mightn't notice that her heart was beating at an alarming rate. The whole situation was so dangerous. A look, an accidental brushing of his hand, and her heart could completely over-rule her head. Even now, in spite of everything, it would still be so easy to forget her pride and plead for the chance to start again. But then, as Morgan had so rightly pointed out, with a man like Grant, there was no second chance.

He sat down at the desk, his face in shadow but his hand resting on the edge in the pool of light thrown by the lamp. She spoke before he could begin. 'I don't know what you want to say, but before you say anything, I want to tell you that I'm leaving.'

'I see!' Fingers that had been curling the edge of a production schedule abruptly stopped. 'To go to your fiancé, I presume?'

'No.' It was out before she could stop it. Far from leaving because of Ramsay, she hadn't thought of him in days. What more proof did she need that she could never marry him? Another victory for the man watching her from the shadow behind the light. How right he'd been when he had accused her of using Ramsay as a shield for her emotions; a protection against the insidious hope, flickering long after all hope should have died, that while her marriage still existed, it could one day be brought back to life.

'But you still want to leave?'

'Yes.' Repeated often enough, it would become a fact.

'I see.' There was a pause. Should she get up and go, or not? 'Would it change your mind if I told you that I loved you?'

An earthquake hit her. Her chair rocked and the floor curved in a series of wavy lines. The sensation faded, leaving her panicky and wide-eyed, filled at first with stunned incomprehension and then with mounting angry disbelief. Grant's face was in the shadow behind the lamp, but in her mind's eye she could see it—strong planes and shadows, an eyebrow lifted mockingly under a thin white ridge of scar, a sensuous mouth curved in a smile and cobalt eyes. Even now, he was determined to have the last word, taunting her with a love that belonged to someone else.

She stood up, gripping both arms of her chair for balance. 'I would think myself a fool if I believed you!' The floor was reassuringly solid beneath her feet and she let go of the chair. 'What is love to you, Grant? The last woman in your bed; the last one you made love to?' Her voice cracked. 'But perhaps one woman isn't enough for you! Perhaps you think Morgan and I are interchangeable!'

He got slowly to his feet, his face everything she had imagined except that now, instead of twisted mocking humour, it was filled with anger. No—more than anger. It was filled with rage. At last she had touched one of *his* raw spots. 'What the hell do you mean?' he demanded thickly.

'Poor Morgan!' She ignored him; her turn for taunting. 'I wonder if she knows that when she's away, you feel free to fill her place with someone else!'

'Stop that!' He gripped her with a grip that almost broke her wrist. 'Morgan has nothing to do with this!'

'Really?' She ignored the pain shooting along her arm and used her voice to goad him; keeping it light and deliberately full of mockery. 'And why's that, I wonder? Because she isn't here! How many other women are there going to be before you next see her? One? Two? Or won't you even bother to keep count?'

'I warn you . . .!' Against the background of dark shadows in the unlit corners, he was powerful and threatening, but, far from stopping her, fear spurred her on.

'What is it, Grant? One rule for you to live by and one for everybody else? Well, let me tell you something.' She could see herself reflected in his eyes, humiliated beyond caring, her face full of unshed tears. 'I lied when I told you Ramsay wasn't my lover. That last weekend at Masseyville, remember? We had two nights alone in the house before you came down. Do you want to hear the details—or can you guess?'

'Damn you, Lissa!' Grant stopped her with a growl deep in his throat before his lips came punishingly down on hers. For a moment she weakened, letting her head fall back under the furious pressure of his assault and thinking of nothing except the sheer physical arousal of his kiss. But gradually she stiffened. Did he really think that by making love to her he would make her forget? That by taking her gently in his arms, as he was doing now, he could send her into the mindless oblivion in which so many of their arguments had ended in the past? She forced her hands up against his chest, ignoring the warmth and hardness beneath the smooth wool of his shirt, and pushed herself away.

'Stop making a fool of me!' she blazed. 'It won't work. Stop using me and checking up on me. Do what you want about a divorce, but just get out of my life!'

CHAPTER TEN

BARBADOS! The shoreline was always perfect at this time of the morning with the sun turning sky from grey to pink to pinkish opalescent green and then, in a few more minutes, when it had pulled itself clear of the horizon, to a brilliant, unvaried blue. A fisherman was already out on the ocean, standing like a black statue in the prow of his small boat, casting his net in graceful, circular motions so that the mesh fell like raindrops on the smooth water. In the distance, the hotel beaches were silent and deserted, the tourists not having yet shaken themselves free of the effects of late-night dancing to the steel bands and a languid swell was coming in and curving, uninterrupted, to spend itself on the shoreline with a quiet sigh.

Walking barefoot along the sand, Lissa Benson Ferries saw none of it. She had come back to the island, but whenever she relaxed control over her mind, she was two thousand miles away. They would have finished filming now and be back in Toronto for the few studio scenes and the post-production work. Norris, Sandy, the secretary who would have been hired to take her place and—her mind baulked, but she forced it on—and Grant.

'Hi, there!' Her thoughts had taken her farther than she had intended: to the seaside frontage of the first hotel. She glanced up and her stomach jack-knifed as memory bridged nine years and made it yesterday. A tall, fair-haired man was coming down the steps from the terrace of the first hotel—but it wasn't Grant. As he got closer, she wondered how she could ever, for an instant, have thought it was. The resemblance was no more than superficial. Blond hair but without that vital crispness; broad shoulders but without that hint of power and eyes that, far from overshadowing it, were no more than a pale echo of the Caribbean stretching ahead of them. A package-dealer, arrived recently, judging from the angry red of too much sun too soon across his face and shoulders, looking for a romance that would last him through a two-week holiday.

'Hi!' He came up to her.

'Good morning.' Lissa went on walking, but he either failed to notice or chose to ignore her obvious lack of interest.

He fell into step beside her. 'Nice place.' She didn't answer. 'You don't mind if I walk along with you for a bit, do you? I'm new here,' he confirmed, 'flew in yesterday.'

She stopped and faced him. 'I'm sorry—I have to go.' She saw the beginnings of a hurt expression as she turned and began to walk quickly back along the beach, but she wasn't the Barbados Tourist Board, she was Lissa Ferries, hurt and in no mood for memories.

She had come back to Barbados because it had seemed the obvious thing to do. London held nothing for her; the Masseys were still in Hawaii and, even if they weren't, the risk of meeting Ramsay made it impossible for her to go back to the ranch. She could never again pretend that he had ever been anything more to her than a futile effort to blot Grant out of her life and she had no idea where he was. In Calgary, presumably, pursuing his career. There had been no word, nothing; since he had presented her with his ultimatum that morning Grant had flown down to the ranch and then walked out of her life.

So she had come back home to an atmosphere that was so strained that even her normally impervious father noticed it. Somehow, in the time she had been away, she and her parents had lost the art of easy communication and, after a first difficult conversation about why she had come back to them, they had gone to pains to avoid the subject of her divorce. It was hard for them, she realised; she might have first claim on their love, but their loyalty would always be split between her and Grant.

She walked up the flight of wooden steps to the pink-washed bungalow above the beach and pushed open the screen door. A letter sat ostentatiously in the middle of the kitchen table. She picked it up, read the address and opened it. It was from her solicitor. The discovery hearing for her divorce was set for the following week. This time, Grant had not refused or changed his mind. She closed her eyes and felt slightly sick.

'Lissa!' Her mother's voice came through the open doorway and when Lissa opened her eyes, Lily Benson was coming along the hall towards her with a look of carefully contructed disinterest on her face. 'There's a letter for you, dear.'

Lissa held it out. 'Yes, I saw.'

'Oh . . . yes.' There was an awkward pause and then her mother went across to one of the old-fashioned kitchen cupboards—never replaced by the modern formica unit she so longed for—and started hunting through the shelves. 'I know it was somewhere here,' she said eventually. 'The big cut glass vase. Darling, have you seen it? It's my turn to have the Bridge Club this afternoon and. . . .'

Lissa smiled. 'It's okay, Mother. You can ask!'

Her mother turned and Lissa saw the capacity to blush she had inherited stain her cheeks. 'Ask? Ask what?' she said uncomfortably.

'What's in the letter. If you thought it was about the divorce, you were right. The discovery hearing's set for next week.'

'I see.' Suddenly older and deflated, her mother sat down at the kitchen table, abandoning all pretence of looking for a vase. 'And then it will all be over?'

'Except for the actual court hearing—yes.' Lissa forced herself not to look away.

'Darling!' Lily's voice was pleading. 'Are you sure you're sure—about the divorce, I mean? Grant's always seemed so much in love with you. All those phone calls and all the times he came to see us after . . . well, I mean, after. . . .' she stopped helplessly.

'After I walked out on him!' Lissa supplied, welcoming the small surge of anger this piece of information about Grant's visits always brought. It had slipped out on her first night home; her mother trying to prove how much he cared.

While she had been thinking she had been making a new life for herself, he had been checking up on her; spying, following her every step. No wonder he had known where to find her in Masseyville—and as for Ramsay, he must have known about him, too. She had mentioned Ramsay in her letters home and Grant had used her parents' distress over the break-up of their marriage and their fondness and admiration for their film star son-in-law to find out everything.

'Darling, don't look so cross!' Her mother looked distressed. 'We would have told you, but Grant was so anxious not to have you know.'

'I'm sure he was!' Lissa muttered underneath her breath. She had gone over his possible reasons time and time again, and one stood out with absolute clarity. A divorce court had to be satisfied that there had been at least some attempt at reconciliation before a marriage could be dissolved. By checking on her whereabouts, Grant had made sure that when *he* decided he wanted a divorce—when

someone like Morgan came into his life—there
would be no time lost in attempting a reconciliation. And she had even provided him with an additional benefit. In agreeing to work for him, she
had supplied the stimulus of rivalry to make his
pursuit of Morgan that much easier. She leaned
across the kitchen table and kissed her mother's
cheek. 'Don't worry,' she said quietly, 'it doesn't
make any difference. Whether Grant knew where I
was or not, the result would have been the same.'

It was hard to get through the next few days
until the hearing, knowing Grant would also be
there to dissect the bare bones of their marriage.
The lawyer's letter had told her that. A hearing of
discovery to establish the cause of the breakdown
of the marriage with both partners present to be
cross-examined by each other's lawyer. How Grant
must resent the fact! His liberty was going to cost
him one more thing—a day, at least, away from
Toronto where he was editing his precious film.
But at least it wouldn't cost him a day away from
Morgan. She was still in Hollywood.

Lissa dressed carefully on the morning of the
hearing. She was asking nothing from Grant—just
the freedom that, in spite of everything, was still
the last thing that she wanted. Her lawyer had
advised her to ask for maintenance: a token sum,
maybe, a dollar a year, but she had refused. It was
enough that she would never, could never, stop
loving Grant; she had no need of the additional
bond of money. She studied herself in her bedroom
mirror. A woman with auburn hair in a lime green

linen suit; cool, composed and perfectly capable of taking on the challenge of life alone.

Her lawyer met her at the entrance to the court house. 'Ready?' he asked.

She swallowed. 'Yes. Will it take long?'

'It shouldn't. Once your husband has arrived. . . .' His eyes went across her shoulder, and she turned. A car was drawing up. She was terrified. She had never been so terrified in her life.

A short fat man she had never seen before got out and, behind him, Grant. He came up the steps towards her. She supposed his lawyer was coming with him, but she could see no one else. There had been no publicity about the hearing: Ferries versus Ferries—with so few people even knowing about their marriage, the local press had not associated the name and Grant had taken none of his usual precautions against recognition. The mane of hair glinting in the sun; the face expressionless above the controlled movement of his body and the eyes holding her in deep, dark shafts of blue.

'Lissa.' He barely acknowledged her, going on from the brilliant sunlight on the steps into the comparatively shadowed interior of the vestibule. She supposed there must have been introductions—his lawyer to hers; hers to his—but all she was conscious of was the man she loved standing so close to her.

The lawyers moved away, discussing some disputed legal point, able to deal unemotionally with the ending of a marriage in which neither of them had been involved.

'Are you satisfied?' His voice took her by surprise.

'Of course. Are you?'

'Of course.' He glanced around the lobby. 'I thought Massey would be with you.'

'Bill? Why should he be here?' Bill Massey was in Hawaii and even if he wasn't, whatever paternal instincts he might have felt towards her did not extend to her asking him to witness this stage of her divorce. She had even refused to allow her parents to come with her.

Grant studied her. 'I thought the name was Ramsay.'

'Yes, of course. How stupid of me!' She tried to cover her mistake. 'Ramsay couldn't be here. He's in. . . .' Her imagination failed and she changed the subject. 'How's Morgan?' she asked brightly.

A shadow of irritation crossed his face. 'Morgan, I presume, is still in Hollywood. Doing the thing that she does best—projecting emotion for the silver screen.'

He was good, she had to give him that. She had flung the question at him and he had fielded it perfectly. It wasn't chance that Grant Ferries had made it to the very top as an actor. It was the ability to hide all his personal feelings and show only what he chose to show.

'How's the film?' Please, she pleaded, please let whatever it was that was delaying them come to an end so that this meaningless, trite interchange could stop and someone—anyone—would come and interrupt them.

'It's good—I think.' For the first time, a flash of the real Grant showed through. 'The rough cut's finished and tomorrow we start dubbing and laying on the tracks.' He paused. 'Did you know you were in it?'

'No.' She looked up and looked away as his eyes locked into hers.

What were they doing here? Carrying on this stilted conversation when, in the far corner, like pin-striped wreckers' men, the two lawyers were amiably discussing the best process of bringing her marriage to an end. She wanted to shout and scream that it was all a terrible mistake. She wanted to wake up and find that it had all been a ghastly dream. Instead, she said, 'Where do I appear?'

'In the sequence with the dogs.' She could still feel him watching her.

'I must have ruined it!'

'No. I'm probably the only one to know you're there. You're one of a crowd of extras watching Massignac go away.'

With Morgan in the foreground, half turned away from camera, also watching him. Lissa could remember that particular shot. It had been one of the first to be done after Grant had brought Morgan back to the set following the incident with the huskies. Torn between the anguish of staying on and watching them together, or going back to the Hen Coop, she had hovered on the edge of camera range and she must have drifted in too close. Her dark, padded coat would have blended in with the crowd players' costumes and for once, even Norris's sharp eye must have missed this extra detail.

'But you can use another take, can't you?' she asked a point somewhere between his chin and the knot of his tie. 'There were two or three, weren't there?'

'Yes,' he agreed. 'But I think I'll keep that one.'

'Oh . . .!' A silence began and lengthened, with Grant as apparently unable or unwilling to break it as she was herself.

All she could think of was that this was the last time she was going to see him. There was no need for him to attend the actual court hearing, and with so much work waiting for him in Toronto—to say nothing of Morgan in Hollywood—a second trip to Barbados would be the last thing he wanted. Without raising her eyes above the tanned skin of his throat, she began to build a mental picture that would last her for a lifetime. She didn't have his image on a few feet of film; she just had memory. She knew she would never be able to bring herself to watch him on the screen again.

Blond hair; yes, she could remember that, and the way it had curled around them like a living, vital thing whenever she had run her fingers through it. She clenched her fingers at her side, forestalling their involuntary movement. Then there were the darker brows and lashes; the heavy lids, often hiding the thoughts reflected on the cobalt surface of his eyes, and the faint white line of the old scar going up into his hairline. His mouth—she shut her eyes as her heart contracted.

It was hopeless to try and build an image piecemeal when she already had so many total memories. Grant laughing, his whole face alive with huge enjoyment; Grant smiling down at her as they made love, the dull sheen of his shoulders marking the perimeter of her world. And then there were the other pictures imprinted on her mind: less happy ones. Grant angry and contemptuous, trying to explain when she shut her ears; Grant with Morgan in his arms. She heard a noise and quickly opened her eyes.

A door was opening and she could see a court stenographer sitting in an adjoining room behind a stenorette machine. At last they were going to begin.

The lawyers stopped talking and came towards them, dividing into separate camps, but, as she went to go to hers, Grant's hand came out and stopped her.

'Lissa!' There was a rough edge to his edge. 'It doesn't have to end like this.'

She looked up at him, shock draining the blood from her face and turning it paper white. How else was a marriage supposed to end? She began to shiver under the pressure of his fingers. What did he want? Friendship? Did he expect her to wish him happiness with Morgan?

'Please!' She felt sick and utterly defeated. 'Let go of me! It's over. There's nothing more to say.'

With a job found for her by an old friend of her father's, it was just a matter of waiting out the weeks until the actual divorce hearing once the hearing for discovery was over. And with that now behind her, she supposed she was half free; just as she was half alive. Going through the motions of normal, everyday existence; eating, sleeping, driving backwards and forwards into Bridgetown and smiling at the people who came into the insurance office.

At home, the atmosphere was even more strained, with long tense silences across the dinner table or else bright, meaningless conversations about safe subjects like her mother's bridge club or her father's books. She had taken to going out on to the gallery at the back of the bungalow after dinner, escaping with a book in her hands to sit and rock slowly back and forth in the old white-painted swing. But no plot, however riveting, could hold her attention and, more often than not, she just sat there, conscious of the night sounds of the tropics and trying not to think.

She was sitting there on the last evening before the hearing when she heard the telephone followed by the sound of footsteps. The phone stopped and she heard her mother's voice. Then, 'Lissa!' Her name came clearly through the screen door. 'It's for you. Hurry, dear, it's overseas!'

Her stomach clenched. An overseas call could only mean one person, but her mother's face held no clue when she handed over the receiver and went back into the living room.

'Hallo!' Her voice was cracked and barely audible. She bit her cheeks to get moisture in her mouth and tried again. 'Hallo!'

'Hi there! How are you?' A woman answered her. A young woman, bubbling over even through the slight echo on the line.

Lissa let her breath out in a ragged sigh. 'Sandy?' she said doubtfully.

'That's right! I'm in Toronto. Hi! How are you?'

'I'm fine. How are you?'

'Just great! Except that as of now, I'm one of the world's great unemployed. The film's finished—or at least my part in it has. We've just been out for a few drinks to celebrate.'

Lissa smiled. That explained the bubbly voice. 'I hope you're not thinking of looking for work down here,' she warned. 'We don't have too much call for continuity girls.'

'No, I don't expect you have,' Sandy said cheerfully. 'But that's not why I'm calling. I had to come back to the studio to pick up my things, so I thought before I left, I'd rip them off for a long-distance call and find out how you were. So,' she went on, 'how are things?'

'They're fine.' Lissa wished she could stop saying that.

'That's great! We were all a bit worried about you, you know—taking off so suddenly.'

'I had family problems.'

'Oh, I see.' Sandy paused. 'Is everything okay now?'

'Yes, it's fi. . . .' Lissa caught herself just in time. 'It's just about settled.' Or would be the next day when the divorce hearing was over. 'What are you working on next?' she asked to change the subject.

'Nothing yet—but something will turn up. It always does!' Sandy replied philosophically. 'But that wasn't what I called to talk about.' Lissa could almost see her expectant smile. 'What I really wanted to know was what you thought about the news?'

'News? What news?' She still didn't guess, still had no idea.

'Don't you know? Morgan's married Norris! It's all over the magazine section of the *Star* tonight. A quiet wedding in Beverly Hills. Except for four million photographers and press agents, of course! You should have seen the pictures. Morgan all virginal in white—virginal, my foot!' Sandy added scathingly. 'And Norris wearing that crazy cap of his! Still, Morgan should care what he looks like. She's in work for life now she's got a husband with a foot inside the door at Universal—or at least she's in work for as long as they stay married . . .!'

Sandy went on, but Lissa was no longer listening. In the warmth of the evening, there was cold sweat on her face and the telephone was slippery. What had she done? On the basis of a few rumours and suspicions, she had thrown everything away. Morgan hadn't spent the nights on location in Grant's trailer; she had been with Norris. And Grant hadn't made love to *her* out of a spirit of revenge, he had made love to her because he wanted her. The thoughts spilled disjointedly through her head.

She should have guessed. She should have

known! His ability to totally switch his mind and energies from one thing to another had always been so much a part of him: what else had she expected that morning in the hotel? That he would have behaved like a moonstruck adolescent while the pressures of time and money wasting were building up in him. He had expected her to be adult enough to understand. Just as he had expected her to be adult on all those other occasions when blind jealousy had made it impossible for her to accept the demands of his career. And then, when she had finally reached breaking point, he had let her go—and waited.

His contact with her parents; his insistence on dragging an entire film crew to Masseyville when Ramsay's name had begun to crop up in her letters home—it all made an awful sort of sense. That morning in Masseyville, when he had stopped her, his hand on her elbow, his eyes boring down into. hers, could have been the moment of their new beginning. Instead, she had destroyed everything.

'Lissa! Lissa! Are you still there . . . Operator! Operator!'

The wild clicking of the telephone in her ear brought her back to the reality of her parents' hallway and the tree frogs chirruping outside. 'It's okay, Sandy, I'm still here.'

'I thought we'd been cut off.' Sandy sounded relieved. 'But listen, I should go. It may not be costing me anything, but this phone call's costing the company a bomb! We'll see you some time, perhaps?'

'Yes—perhaps.' It wasn't likely. Some friendships went on after work was finished; others ended with the job. This might, or might not, have been one of the second sort, but Sandy was firmly rooted in the film world and all its gossip, and Lissa doubted if she would ever set foot in that particular world again.

'Take care, then.' Sandy seemed to sense the unlikelihood of them ever meeting again in the future and her voice had a downward beat.

'Yes . . . take care. And thanks for calling.' Lissa slowly replaced the receiver. What did she do now? Go to bed, she thought, and then tomorrow drive into Bridgetown and get her divorce.

The papers were full of it the following morning— or at least, the gossip pages. Grainy pictures of Morgan and Norris gazing lovingly at each other against a background of a Californian garden. Someone in the local editorial office had also remembered Morgan's one and only visit to Barbados nine years earlier. It was enough to give the little island a vested interest in an international story, and there was another picture of Morgan, in a mini-skirt, coming down the steps of a plane at Seawell airport. The caption underneath went farther; linking her name with Grant's as a past romance, and that, Lissa supposed, was why there were photographers and reporters in a solid group around the steps when she finally arrived outside the courthouse building.

From the Ferries in Morgan's past to the name

on the list of uncontested divorces down for that day's hearing was hardly too great a jump for an editor with a sixth sense about what might be happening.

'It's out, I'm afraid.' Her lawyer hurried to meet her as she stood uncertainly on the fringes of the group wondering what to do. 'Come on, I'll get you through.'

'Mrs Ferries!' For all the confidence in the voice, it was still a question rather than a statement. There had been no publicity about her marriage; Grant had not been a film star then and the reporter aggressively thrusting a microphone in front of her could not be certain who she was. He was probably asking everyone.

'Will you please stop bothering my client?' the lawyer snapped without pausing, his hand on Lissa's elbow urging her through. Undecided, the crowd of journalists stood back. 'Right, we're nearly there.' The lawyer's whisper was almost lost in a sudden ripple of excitement as a car pulled up at the kerb. The reporters flocked towards it and Lissa heard flashbulbs popping and the high-pitched competition of shouted questions.

She stopped in the courthouse doorway and turned to look, her heart thumping and her throat dry. It couldn't be! He had no need to be there. He wouldn't have flown two thousand miles to witness the ending of something that she had irrevocably destroyed.

The car door opened and Grant got out. Unshaven, with all the signs of having flown straight through the night, nothing could detract from a look that pierced the crowds and locked straight on to her.

'Grant! Mr Ferries! Hey, Grant—this way!' The competition for his attention reached fever pitch as he walked slowly up the steps. 'Have you got a comment? Will you tell us why you're here?' One voice, more persistent than the rest, rose above the noise.

'Sure!' He smiled his famous smile and paused. 'Make it a headline,' he suggested. 'I've come to stop my wife making the biggest mistake of my life!'

There must have been questions shouted and flashbulbs popping as he took her in his arms and the reporters jostled to get the stories and the pictures that would go by wire service around the world, but Lissa saw and heard none of it. All she could feel was the possessive pressure of his body as he drew her close to him and the strobing flash of lights was in her head as he searched for the answer to his unasked question in her upturned face.

'Will you come back to me?' When it did come, the question was no more than a vibration against her lips, part of a kiss that sent spirals of happiness reaching for her heart as his love poured out to claim her and make her his.

She was back. She was home. She was where she had always been meant to be.

'Oh, yes,' she sighed. 'Oh, yes!'

We value your opinion...

You can help us make our books even better by completing and mailing this questionnaire. Please check [✓] the appropriate boxes.

1. Compared to romance series by other publishers, do Harlequin novels have any additional features that make them more attractive?

   1.1 ☐ yes   .2 ☐ no   .3 ☐ don't know

   If yes, what additional features? _____

   _____

   _____

2. How much do these additional features influence your purchasing of Harlequin novels?

   2.1 ☐ a great deal .2 ☐ somewhat .3 ☐ not at all .4 ☐ not sure

3. Are there any other additional features you would like to include?

   _____

   _____

   _____

4. Where did you obtain this book?

   4.1 ☐ bookstore   .4 ☐ borrowed or traded
   .2 ☐ supermarket   .5 ☐ subscription
   .3 ☐ other store   .6 ☐ other (please specify)_____

5. How long have you been reading Harlequin novels?

   5.1 ☐ less than 3 months   .4 ☐ 1-3 years
   .2 ☐ 3-6 months   .5 ☐ more than 3 years
   .3 ☐ 7-11 months   .6 ☐ don't remember

6. Please indicate your age group.

   6.1 ☐ younger than 18 .3 ☐ 25-34   .5 ☐ 50 or older
   .2 ☐ 18-24   .4 ☐ 35-49

Please mail to: **Harlequin Reader Service**

In U.S.A.
1440 South Priest Drive
Tempe, AZ 85281

In Canada
649 Ontario Street
Stratford, Ontario N5A 6W2

Thank you very much for your cooperation.

Readers all over the country say Harlequin is the best!

"You're #1."

A.H.*, Hattiesburg, Missouri

"Harlequin is the best in romantic reading."

K.G., Philadelphia, Pennsylvania

"I find Harlequins are the only stories on the market that give me a satisfying romance, with sufficient depth without being maudlin."

C.S., Bangor, Maine

"Keep them coming! They are still the best books."

R.W., Jersey City, New Jersey

*Names available on request.

4 FREE

Harlequin Romances

NOW...

8 NEW
Harlequin ◈ *Presents...*
EVERY MONTH!

Romance readers everywhere have expressed their delight with Harlequin Presents, along with their wish for more of these outstanding novels by world-famous romance authors. Harlequin is proud to meet this growing demand with 2 more NEW Presents every month—a total of 8 NEW Harlequin Presents every month!

MORE of the most popular romance fiction in the world!

On sale wherever paperback books are sold.

No one touches the heart of a woman quite like Harlequin.